— ARENA —

John Cranna was born in Te Aroha, New
Zealand, in 1954 and grew up in the Waikato.
He spent a number of years in London, and now
lives in Auckland. His first book, *Visitors*, won
the 1990 New Zealand Book Award for Fiction,
and the 1990 Commonwealth Writers Prize for
Best First Book. *Arena* is his first novel.

John Cranna

— ARENA —

Minerva

A Minerva Paperback
ARENA

First published in Great Britain 1993
by Minerva
an imprint of Reed Consumer Books Limited
Michelin House, 81 Fulham Road, London SW3 6RB
and Auckland, Melbourne, Singapore and Toronto
First published in 1992 by Minerva New Zealand

Copyright © John Cranna 1992

A CIP catalogue record for this title
is available from the British Library
ISBN 0 7493 9858 2

Printed and bound in Great Britain
by Cox and Wyman Limited, Reading, Berks.

To my mother and father

— I —

We came to the city in early summer and made our home beneath a grandstand. In the afternoons we lay beneath the slats and watched the sun cast its reddened bars around us, or made love and talked of how to exorcise her father, who lived, she said, in both of us, although I to my knowledge had never met the man. Sometimes she made love to her father in me, and sometimes I made love to her father in her, and afterwards we lay in the cool earth and listened to the slow kick of new life in her belly.

Jan had come from a home in the south, the unknown south of wide brown plains, apricot trees and running water (or so she said) and when I questioned her more closely on the details of this landscape I had never known, and which belonged, I said, to the stuff of colonial fictions, she looked at me carefully, as though inspecting the pigment of my iris, and put a cool dry hand between my legs. She liked my eyes, she said, she liked the distance between them, which she said was unusually great. Her own eyes were unremarkable except for the fact that they were of different colours, blue and green, something that was quite difficult to establish in the dim light beneath the grandstand, if I sometimes doubted the truth of this, which I did. It had been hard as a girl to be taken seriously with those eyes, she told me, she had been considered something of a freak in the distant playgrounds of her childhood. On other aspects of my own body, in which she took a lot of interest on those long afternoons, she was less complimentary. It seemed that in some respects I suffered by comparison with her father.

You can see that I'm prone to doubt the word of my lover, here in our home beneath the grandstand, but this shouldn't be taken to reflect so much on her. It's true that at that time in my life, before the Birth and everything that followed, I was certain of very little. What trust I had in things was often misplaced. I was unable, for whatever reason, to pick a liar. In such a state, how much credence would you give to someone with different-coloured eyes?

Our first weeks were spent in mapping out the stadium and its neighbourhood. We moved about only at night, unsure of our status in the area and uncertain of how long it would take the caretaker of the stadium to discover our presence there, keen to avoid anything that would risk the security of our new home. The caretaker was a thin, angry man, who took his job very seriously and would certainly attempt to catch us as soon as he discovered intruders in his territory. In anticipation of this, we made note of the likely points for the setting of traps, and were careful to watch the ground for signs of fresh digging. In the mornings we observed him through cracks in the grandstand as he shovelled the stained sand from last season's festivities into a drum and took it away on his tractor. Stripped to the waist, he worked with absolutely regular movements, the sweat running on his sallow skin. At the end of the day he came back with the cleaned sand and spread it around the arena with a shovel.

The daily rituals of the caretaker were a comfort to us (at least until his rituals began to take account of us), we craved their order after our months of travel, the nights spent in different locations, the days of constantly shifting landscapes. We noted everything about him, the economical arc of his shovel, the leather boots with polished toe-caps, the head shaven like a convict's. We observed his little habits, the way he re-tied his bootlaces every hour or so for no particular reason, and the

10

fingering of the beads in his pocket before beginning work on the sand at the start of every day.

My lover coveted those boots of his and dreamed about them at night. In the mornings she spoke of marathon walks that carried her across stones and burning sand to a stream where she removed the boots and washed her feet in cool water. I asked her whether her dreams included the means by which she obtained the boots from their owner, but she said they did not. Her own footwear amounted to a pair of sandals which had served her for as long as she could remember and which clung to her feet as shreds of leather.

'Soon,' she said, touching her belly, 'I'll have to have proper boots. And those are the only ones around.' I looked out at the caretaker, at his hard stringy body, and hoped I would not have to take his boots by force.

At night we left the stadium in search of food, and travelled a kilometre to the beginnings of a Guest suburb where there was plenty to be had for the taking. Our main competitors were the packs of dogs who came up from the river at dusk, but in general they foraged in the loose refuse and left us first pickings from the plastic sacks that lay along the roadways. We slit these sacks with a long-bladed knife and extracted the remains of the mutton-birds that the Guests were eating that Christmas. The carcasses were wrapped in foil and there was usually still plenty of flesh on the bones. Last year it had been some other bird, and next year it could just as easily be new-born foals. The culinary fashions of the Guests were as unpredictable as everything else about them.

We placed these foil bundles in a canvas bag that my lover carried on her back, and when we had filled the bag, we hurried to the stadium before the dogs from the river managed to catch the scent of the food we had stolen from under their noses. Back in our home beneath the grandstand we opened the parcels and spread out the foil as a table-cloth. There were three of us to feed, and the life that grew in the belly of my lover had an

11

appetite as big as the already born. We divided the food into three equal portions and my lover ate two of them, and afterwards we used crusts to scoop up the fat from the foil, but even then we were not certain that we had satisfied the appetite of the creature within her.

The caretaker lived in a house behind the stadium, a run-down affair with a ramshackle veranda that we passed at night on our way out to gather food. After his daily efforts in the stadium he seemed to have no energy left to expend on his own house and the rust was beginning to show through the unpainted iron of the roof. He lived by himself, as far as we could tell, and tended a plot of vegetables behind his house which was surrounded by banana palms to conceal it from free gatherers like us. On our way home with our bag of mutton-birds at midnight we paused to lift a few vegetables from this plot, taking care to remove the bare minimum and to leave the soil undisturbed, so as not to arouse his suspicions.

As generous in her dreams as she was in the waking world, my lover included the caretaker in our suppers gathered from the refuse bags of the rich. In the mornings she spoke of a handsome table at which the caretaker took his place beside us, dressed for the occasion in a starched white shirt with the collar buttoned close to his neck. His hands, she said, were dry and perfectly formed and he removed the flesh from the bones of our captured birds with the elegance of a surgeon.

After waking, when I looked out on the grey irascible man, bent to his task over the hot sand of the arena, I wondered at my lover's dreams, at this other world she inhabited when she closed her odd-coloured eyes each night, and at the scenes she witnessed there. My own nights had for many years been free of dreams, as bland as the shadow that fell across the stadium at dusk, something that my lover thought scarcely possible and mocked in me as a disability. Meanwhile she scooped up her mutton-bird fat, dreamed her dreams and examined the pigment of my iris with the same easy confidence, as though to prove her former life on the wide brown plains of the south was the fiction I suspected it to be, and she had been born and bred to live in dark places in the decaying heartlands of northern cities.

Returning from our food-gathering one night, a little clumsy with tiredness, I broke the glass in a cloche the caretaker had set up in his garden. Immediately the light went on in his bedroom. As we hurried away through the screen of banana palms a window overlooking the garden was thrown up. When we reached our home the flap of our canvas bag was loose and we found that we had lost two mutton-birds. In the morning the caretaker went about his routines as before, and when we ventured out again late that evening Jan found one of the bundles amongst the palms near the garden. As a precaution we decided to avoid the garden for a time. We missed the peppers and avocados from the caretaker's garden, and without them grew quickly tired of our diet of greasy birds. After four days we ventured back into the garden. As a consequence my lover came very close to being crippled.

We had waited until after midnight, and observed the house from the edge of the banana palms before making our way through the tall foliage towards the garden. The night was very quiet apart from the occasional distant bark from the direction of the river. Jan was beside me, a hand on my elbow, when a trap shut close by with a sound like a whip. For a moment I was uncertain of the origin of the noise, and then my lover knelt down abruptly, put her head in her hands and remained there crouched rigid on the grass for several minutes. I saw the teeth of the device like a living thing in the undergrowth, where it had been concealed among broken palms.

In the cool of our home we discussed our relations with the caretaker. Jan examined her fingernails and said in a slow voice that he had broken unwritten rules; that capture, even violent

13

punishment, was expected by free gatherers, but that force of the kind he had attempted to use against us, lethal force, was something different. I said that I doubted the caretaker had any idea of our identity, that he might very well believe we were dogs from the river, but Jan laughed a hard dry laugh that echoed in the confined space of our home.

'River dogs don't eat avocados,' she said. We sat in silence for a while and then I said, 'There's nothing we can do.' Jan lay back on the earth, placed a hand on her belly and stared up at the framework of the grandstand. She said no more about the trap that evening or for several days afterwards, but I knew that the incident continued to prey on her and I wondered whether the caretaker was still invited to the dinner table of her dreams.

Outside, the heat of the summer was mounting, and we watched the caretaker's sallow skin turn brown as he worked the glittering sands of the stadium. Over the course of our stay beneath the grandstand he had moved only a small fraction of the sand, and I calculated he would not be finished until May if his work rate did not increase. The new season began at Easter, and I wondered what would happen to him if he had not completed his work by then. I thought that as an aging man he might be shown tolerance, perhaps even allocated an assistant, but when I discussed this with my lover she shook her head and said that she thought it more likely that he would be made an example of and included in the games himself.

With the Christmas festivities of the Guests drawing to an end and the supplies of birds drying up, we were obliged to go further afield in search of food. Much of our food was still taken from the refuse sacks in the Guest suburb but now we ventured further south along the river to the edge of the slums, where the odd fruit tree grew wild in a vacant lot and the gardens were less expertly fenced and easier to get into. Since the incident with the trap we had stayed away from the caretaker's garden, but my lover craved fruit and vegetables nonetheless, and it was now the dusty gardens of the poor we stole from, with their diseased vegetables and straggling vines and the occasional mangy guard dog which we fed mutton-bird bones to silence.

But the caretaker was more persistent than we had imagined and a little later we noticed signs of fresh digging near the entrance to our home. On careful inspection we found a gin-trap concealed beneath a canopy of fine mesh and earth. We knew now that the caretaker had a fair idea of our location, that he knew us to be human intruders and that he took our presence in his domain seriously. We sat with a candle between us that night and discussed the next step. Jan was angry now, her cheeks white beyond the flame, her fist a ball in her lap.

'We have to get him before he gets one of us,' she said. I said that it would be unwise to attempt violence against him — even if we were to succeed, we would only attract the attention of his superiors. We had two clear choices, I said. We either left the stadium immediately, or accepted the risks and remained continuously alert. My lover sat watching the candle for an hour, then abruptly snuffed the flame, lay down and slept. That night I heard her moving in her dreams, murmuring to herself in the opaque language of sleep and once she cried out in a dead voice, but when I tried to wake her she turned away and retreated deeper into her nightmare.

At dawn she got up and went out alone, her face pale but with marks of high colour in her cheeks. She returned soon afterwards with the gin-trap and placed it carefully in the bag we used to collect our food.

'Did you cover the hole?' She nodded and settled down on her stomach to watch the caretaker at his tasks. We observed him for many hours that day without a word passing between us, mesmerised by the gleaming shovel and the thump of sand on the trailer. For the first time I caught his scent, which was blown towards our hiding place by a light wind, the thin sour smell of old men who live alone, mixed with the sweat of his exertions.

By dusk I knew that we must act, we could not stay here waiting for our keeper to snare us like animals. Neither could we run, it was too late for that, we had made our stake beneath the grandstand and with the creature inside her now we could not go back to our life on the road.

The caretaker kept his tools in a shed beneath the main stand at the far end of the ground, and that night we went out with the gin-trap in our bag and walked around the stadium to the tool-shed. The padlock was old and gave after several sharp blows with a stone. We took a spade and a shovel from amongst the tools, together with a sheet of fine mesh and some oil for the trap. Each morning the caretaker took the same route to his work — from his house to the shed, then on to where his tractor was parked by the wall of the main stand. We began the pit half-way along the path to the tool-shed.

The ground had been baked by the sun, and I had to return to the shed for a pick to break up the surface crust. Jan oiled the trap and checked its mechanism. When I had finished I set the device and my lover held the mesh across the mouth of the pit while I secured its edges and covered it with a fine layer of earth. There was a half moon, enough light to work by, but not enough to be certain we had completely disguised the pit. When we had done the best we could, we shovelled the excavated earth into our canvas bag and made our way back to the grandstand. We did not sleep that night, and with dawn we listened for the sound of the device being tripped.

The caretaker did not appear that morning, but we heard nothing from the trap and were reluctant to leave the safety of our home until we were certain that he had been incapacitated. At midday the sun beat down on the sand of an empty stadium. We discussed the situation, and decided that we must have missed the sound of the trap. We made our way along the perimeter of the stand, but when we got to the path we found the pit uncovered and the trap gone. We saw no one, and so far as we could tell, no one witnessed our hurried return to the grandstand. Back in our home I said that I thought the caretaker had probably gone to report to his superiors, and that if the Guests became involved we should leave immediately. I had heard, I said, that they were experts in the use of gas.

'They'll flush us out like rats,' I said. My lover looked at me with her mocking odd-coloured eyes.

'Guests — for a couple of scavengers like us?'

She said she thought that he had probably gone to get a crony to help him locate us, perhaps another caretaker from the stadium by the river. 'They'll have a hard job in a place this size,' she said. We agreed to lie low for several days, to live off the small stock of food we had in reserve, and to ensure that one of us was always awake and on watch. I loosened some boards further along the skirting of the grandstand to provide another exit. For days we lived on the few scraps we had in reserve and on the remains of previous meals. We sucked the marrow from discarded mutton-bird bones and chewed the smaller ones to pulp and swallowed the mush.

We saw nothing of the caretaker or anyone else, the digging had stopped, and with our increasing hunger and the light-headedness it brought, our fears about the plans being laid by our keeper grew steadily more intense. By the fifth day we had had enough. My lover could stand her hunger no more, and I knew that lack of food would soon sap our strength to the point where we would be helpless if discovered. An hour or so before dawn, we left the grandstand and made our way to the banana grove. To our surprise, the caretaker's house was lit up as though in expectation of visitors, and panels of light from the windows fell across the garden and into the palms.

From where we stood, the main room of the house was visible through the gaping front door. A huddle of black clothing lay propped against the far wall of the room. For a while the shape appeared formless, but eventually a human figure began to

17

emerge, its back against the wall and its head thrown forward at an odd angle. 'It's him. He's dead,' whispered my lover. But our keeper was not dead, and when we ventured on to the front veranda of his house and stood in the doorway, the lolling head was thrown back and the blank eyes of a cripple looked up at us. The trap, metallic, black, encased his foot and ankle like a rare tumour. Jan bent down beside our keeper and stared into his eyes, as though searching for some resemblance to the urbane guest of her dreams. Then she went out into the kitchen and began to empty the drawers. The man was older than I had imagined, closer to sixty than fifty, and his cheeks showed a fine webbing of blood vessels from years of exposure to the sun. In the lobe of his right ear he carried a small gold stud.

Jan had returned from the kitchen. The caretaker looked up at her with dull eyes. When he saw the carving steel she held, he raised a hand in weak defence, but unable to sustain its weight he let his arm fall to his side again. I saw the sweat start out on the temples of his shaven head. My lover stood looking down at our keeper for a while, then knelt beside him, inserted the steel between the metal jaws and with the smooth movements of a trapper eased the device free of his leg. Then gently, taking great care not to disturb his ankle, she removed the bootlaces from his fine leather boots and slipped them off his feet.

2

Intoxicated with joy at her new possessions, my lover took off all her clothes that night and made love to me in the caretaker's boots. Earlier we had found three jars of home-made cider and drank up two of them while our injured host watched us from the couch of his living-room. We washed his ankle, and unable to find any antiseptic in the house, used the liquor to sterilise his wound. When we had finished the rest of the cider ourselves, my lover began negotiations.

'The Guests will sack you or worse if you can't clean their stadium,' she said to our silent keeper. 'Perhaps we can come to some arrangement?'

We left him on the couch with his hollow eyes and three days of stubble and returned to our burrow. Moving together in the earth beneath the stadium my lover whispered of the creature that quickened within her, of the pain and terror of new life, of blood and death and sex and fear, and when she came she cried out with a harsh animal sound that echoed away among the endless tiers of seats above us. Later, in the dead hours before dawn, she got up in her sleep and tried to walk about in her new boots. For the rest of the night I smoothed her temple and spoke to her while she tossed in a delirium brought on by the cider and the blow to her skull. In the morning she had forgotten everything, and had to be assured that the caretaker was our captive, that he was at our mercy and that it was time for negotiations to recommence.

We fed our keeper and changed his dressings. I made a splint from a length of broom handle, and although his face drained of colour he did not cry out when I straightened and set his ankle. I investigated the house, pacing out the dimensions of each room to confirm the size of our new domain. For reasons that were unclear to me I noted these dimensions with a pencil stub on a piece of paper. Jan stood gazing at the bathroom with its chrome fittings, heated water and smooth tile-lined walls. She spun the tap and watched as steam rose from the running water. In the kitchen we discovered food that left us silent with awe: toheroa soup in cans, case upon case of it, and real butter and loaves of cloying white bread. Our captive watched dully as we stacked up his supplies, suspecting perhaps that having released him from the trap, for our own perverse reasons we were now going to leave him to starve. In fact we piled up the provisions in order to stare at so much food together in one place.

When it was all on the table, we sat on either side of the pile we had made and observed our cache. As a child, said Jan, she had once brought home a quantity of canned soup she had found abandoned on a tip. Her mother had been very angry, and had returned the cans with a warning on the subject of contaminated foods. Unable to bear the loss of her treasure, Jan retrieved the cans and buried them in a corner of the garden. Occasionally she would dig up one of the cans and eat its contents in secret. This, she said, gave her great pleasure. She spoke to our keeper, who was propped in a chair by the stove.

'So you see I've been scavenging from an early age,' she said. The caretaker, whose face had regained some colour since we fed him, looked up at her without expression, then spat deliberately on the floor. My lover picked out a pair of scissors from the kitchen drawer. She went over to our captive and touched the tip of the blade to his ear lobe. She tapped the golden stud.

'What would I get for this at the southern market?' The caretaker regarded her with hard flat eyes but I could tell that he thought her capable of anything, and he kept very still until she returned the scissors to the drawer.

We had washed in streams in the country, but since arriving in the city we had had no opportunity to bathe, and now Jan undressed and lay on her back in our new bath with her lips apart, while I turned the water on her and she lay gasping beneath the needle spray. Even now my lover would not relinquish her boots, and when I tried to tear them from her she cried out in terror, 'Stop stop, they're part of my feet!'

Together in the bath we discussed the hostility of our captive. Jan said that he would realise with time that he had little option but to co-operate. We must make allowances for his pride and for every caretaker's hatred of free gatherers, she said. It was a matter of waiting for him to adjust to the humiliation of defeat. She slid down the bath until her head was below the level of the water. I felt the soft rise in her muscular belly. When she lay still I could detect a steady pulse there, like the stirring of a small but determined heart.

In subsequent days it seemed to me that Jan spent more time in that bright room with tiles and running water than was humanly possible, the water had become her obsession. She lay in the bath for hours at a time, or basked in the needle spray, singing to herself in a melancholy voice that belonged to someone else. She told me that life in the womb was in favour of music, and she demanded that I play my flute to her. The battered instrument had lain untouched amongst our possessions for months. I wondered whether I could remember a simple scale. I sat on the side of the bath and played a stumbling tune that was improved by the acoustics of the bathroom. Jan closed her eyes as though listening to the finest music and very quickly fell asleep.

Although she did not say as much, I sensed that Jan had begun to conserve her energies for the child, and was beginning to withdraw further into the distant world of motherhood. I took responsibility for meals and for the interrogation of our keeper, who seemed no more receptive to my approaches than he had been to my lover's. I washed his wound each day, and checked for signs of infection, although there was little I could do if he became ill. After I had completed this daily ritual, I asked him questions which he did not answer, although he no longer responded by spitting on the floor.

I knew from observation that our keeper was a solitary man, but I thought it likely that he had some regular contact with his employers, and I was concerned that we might be surprised by a visit. After another two days of silence I considered threatening him with the scissors, or starving him until he spoke. For as long as there was a chance of him thawing, however, it seemed wise to use more indirect means. I went through the papers he kept in his living room, but was unable to find anything of interest apart from the fact that our keeper was a subscriber to *Black-Bait* magazine. Arranged along the window-sill in his living room was a collection of odd, stunted plants, and I made a point of watering these daily in the hope that my show of concern might free up his tongue.

After a week or so the caretaker was able to move about a little with the aid of crutches I had fashioned for him from a length of pipe. I took the crutches from him at night to prevent an escape attempt. Now that he was more mobile I decided to put him to work in the garden, and was surprised when he did as I requested. There was weeding to do, and I watched him moving awkwardly across the plot on his knees, his ankle trailing behind him as a useless appendage. I found vegetable seeds in his shed and gave him these to plant, which he did with methodical care.

It was then that he spoke to me for the first time. I went cold at the sound of his voice, which was high and grated in the quiet of the palm-ringed garden. He asked me to fetch some fertiliser from his shed, something he was unable to do himself on his crutches. As I watched him carefully mix the fertiliser into the soil among the seed rows I realised why he was taking so much trouble with the garden. He clearly believed that my lover and I would not be around to benefit from his labours. My anxieties about a visit from his superiors were revived.

At the end of his day in the garden I fetched a fine chain and a padlock from his stores. I looped one end of the chain around the avocado at the edge of his garden and made him lie down. I placed a bight of chain around his good ankle and secured it with the padlock. 'You're sleeping out tonight,' I told him. He looked . up at me blankly with his reptile's eyes.

Although the days were stiflingly hot, the nights were clear and cold and in the morning I went out to see how he had fared. He was huddled beneath the avocado, his clothes wet with dew. I squatted beside him. He drew his hand over his bristly head and looked to where the sun was beginning to show between the banana palms. When he had warmed up I asked again about his superiors. I wanted to know how often they called, and the details of their activities when they came. He moved stiffly with his chain and said nothing. He spent four nights in the garden before I broke his silence.

The Guests, he eventually told me, came every month or so to check on his progress and pay him a bonus if he was on schedule. The next visit was six days away. He said no more than this, and I led him with chattering teeth to the house and ran a bath to reward him for his co-operation. While the caretaker sat in his steaming water I considered what he had said. My lover was convinced that the Guests took no excuses from their employees, and that our keeper's inability to work on the stadium could be the end of his secure caretaker's life. If this was the case, why did he refuse to negotiate with us? We had proposed to the caretaker that I take over his work until he was fit again. The preparation of the stadium was falling further and further behind schedule, and there was every prospect, it seemed, of the caretaker not only losing his job, but ending up in the games himself. In return for help with the cleaning, we wanted protection from enquiries by the Guests, and food and shelter until the creature was born. But we could not force the caretaker into an agreement: he would simply betray us. We had to get him to co-operate of his own accord.

I watched him in the bath as he sponged his chest and arms. His skin was hairless like that of an oriental and, although his face suggested a man in his late fifties, the body was still lean and well-muscled. He turned to look at me through the steam, a shrewd look that suggested for an instant a much younger man, a businessman perhaps who had been advantaged by the first visits, but who had fallen foul of his masters and was now condemned to serve them in another role. He had removed the golden stud from his ear and was soaping his bristly skull. His hands moved in stabbing movements across his head.

'What did you do before this?' I said. He jerked around, and then went back to scrubbing his skull. I repeated my question, more loudly. He pretended that he had not heard, and lathered the soap over his ears. I went out to the kitchen, filled a bucket from the cold tap and returned to the bathroom. By now his entire head was covered with lather. I pitched the contents of the bucket over him and asked my question again. He turned to me slowly. I could see the hatred there; not the hatred of the caretaker for the free-gatherer, but the loathing of the collaborator for his interrogator. I got up and went out of the bathroom.

The following morning, five days before the date given by our keeper, a truck drew up in the driveway outside the house. I was in the garden with the caretaker planting autumn melon seeds and saw the glint of metal through the palms before I heard its engine. I picked up a pair of garden shears and placed the point of them against the cripple's throat. We were concealed from the driveway by the screen of palms but Jan was asleep in the house.

24

The driver turned off the engine, got down from his cab and walked to the front door of our home. He was clad in overalls and carried a clipboard under his arm. The other door of the cab opened and a second man got out. He stood resting his hand on the bonnet of the vehicle.

After waiting for some time at the door, the driver knocked again with greater force. A minute went by, and then the driver turned to his companion and spoke in a low voice. The two of them walked off in the direction of the stadium. Our keeper stared after the men without expression. Ten minutes passed and the pair returned to the vehicle and unfastened its tail-gate. One of them climbed on to the deck of the vehicle and began to prepare its contents for unloading. The truck contained a number of plywood boxes, and it was possible to tell from the ease with which they were handled that the boxes were empty. The men stacked the boxes, a dozen or so in all, beside the house and then the driver returned to the front door and knocked one more time. Eventually he made a few notes on a clipboard, removed the sheet of paper and slipped it under the door. I watched the vehicle back carefully down the drive and move off in the direction of the industrial suburbs to the east. Jan opened the door with caution, dressed in a towel, and looked after the departing vehicle.

Over a plate of steaming toheroa soup that night I put it to the caretaker that he had deceived us, and that he had lost his right to fair treatment. I told him that I was considering chaining him to the tree on a permanent basis. Jan blew on her spoonful of soup.

'We can't be certain he knew about the delivery,' she said. The caretaker tugged at his golden stud, as though to reassure himself that his ear was still intact. My lover smiled at this gesture.

'If you are double-crossing us,' she said, 'we'll cut off more than that.'

Our keeper's face began to stretch in what appeared at first to be a grimace of disgust, but with time I realised that he was trying to control a smile. I watched as the smile increased in intensity until it disfigured his entire face. He began to swallow rapidly, as though choking on his soup. Short sobs came from his throat. Gradually these sobs became louder and it became clear that the caretaker was in fact laughing. He laid his soup spoon in his plate, and unable to control his mirth, started to convulse with a high-pitched sound that racked his whole body. The noise increased in strength until he was overcome by it, a spasm that picked him up and shook him from head to foot. His soup plate overturned and slewed the pale green liquid across the table.

Eventually the spasm petered out in a fit of coughing. Jan gazed at him across the table.

'We didn't know you had a sense of humour,' she said. I fetched a cloth and took the scissors from the drawer. I wiped up the spilled liquid and wrung the cloth over his plate. I motioned to the caretaker to continue with his meal.

'We're interested in the delivery today,' I said. 'We want to know whether there'll be any more.' The cripple sipped at his soup. I placed a hand on the scissors. He spoke suddenly in his strained, reedy voice.

'As the season gets closer there are all sorts of preparations.' He made a distracted gesture with his spoon. 'You know how fussy they are about these things. I'm even supposed to build kennels this year. They have some plan to bring in river dogs.' He paused, as though concerned that he had said too much. I picked up the scissors. The cripple's voice rose in pitch.

'I don't know about the deliveries. How can I know?' He spread his hands. 'Look at last year. They decide at the last moment they want a marsupial dog. Three days before the games I get a freezer full of offal and some animal technician here all day teaching me how to look after marsupial dogs. How to keep them hungry but not too hungry.' He grimaced. 'Anyway, these delivery people aren't interested in your kind. I told you when

26

the Guests are due. You've interfered with their preparations. They won't like that.'

'We think they'll be upset with you, too.' Anxiety touched the caretaker's expression for a moment and then was gone. 'The Guest looks after his Host,' he said in a monotone. My lover laughed a hard, cold laugh.

'I haven't heard that for a long time,' she said. 'Where have you been for the last ten years?'

The following morning my lover did not get out of bed. She complained of nausea and turned her head to the wall. I stroked her hair and touched the film of sweat that coated her forehead. Her mouth tasted of ashes, she said, and her cunt ached of the grave. I bent over her and saw that her eyes were no longer different colours, they had become the same dull emerald and in that instant I knew she was dying, but then the illusion passed and I saw that I had been the victim of a trick of the light. I wiped her forehead with a cool cloth and left her to sleep.

In the afternoon she was no better and I played her a tune on the flute, a piece I recalled from my childhood, but after a while she moved fitfully in the bed and put a hand to her temple as though the music caused her pain. I went to the window and looked towards the city. In the garden our keeper crawled like an insect — brooding, I thought, on murderous plans while he prepared his seed-beds and pulled at the weeds that sprouted amongst the young plants. A yellow haze obscured the horizon from the slums of the south to the Guest suburbs in the north. The discoloured skies would not clear until there was rain, but there had been nothing for weeks and the summer limped on in the same still, penetrating heat.

As dusk fell Jan complained of cramps and I worried that her labour was about to start, but I knew that she was not due for some time yet and that the creature could not survive if it were born now. Although I was ignorant of the process of birth, I thought that some sort of spasms signalled the beginning of labour and Jan showed no signs of these. She lay limp and exhausted in the bed. She whispered that the pain had spread through her body and I pulled back the damp sheets, stroked her skin and told her that she had a passing fever and that she would be well in a few days. I placed my hand on her belly to search for the movement of that other heart, and felt the delicate tread, faint but steady, waiting in the darkness, not ready yet to move into the outside world. I lay beside my lover while she drifted back into sleep, watching the square of yellow sky beyond the window turn slowly to a deep khaki.

After a while I dozed off, and what seemed a little time later I woke with a start in the darkened room. The air had become very cold. My head was clear but there was a faint hum in my ears and the room seemed to have expanded with the coming of night. At the window a shadow was marked against the sky. I watched it for some time, trying to focus in the gloom. Then Jan stirred in her sleep and the shadow moved from the window and the dull glint of a gold ear-ring told me that our keeper had watched us as we slept.

Next day Jan's breathing was thin and rasping with the fever. I watched her during the morning and at intervals I changed the cloth I had placed on her forehead. At midday, I went to the stadium and walked out into the middle of the arena. The sand stretched away from me in a dazzling sweep. A tide-mark ran across the arena about a third of the way down its length, marking the point at which we had trapped the caretaker and the cleaning had stopped. Here in the centre of the arena clouds of bright blue flies hung low above the sand, and as I watched, a small swarm separated itself from the main mass and came to investigate the intruder. In an instant I was surrounded by the insects, which bit at my face and hands, but which just as quickly were gone.

Before me, at a position half-way up the tiers of seats, was the ministerial box, with its windows of blank glass and its ugly insignia. Directly beneath this box was a system of gates and passageways that led back under the grandstand. The gates opening into the arena were made of the same bright metal, which reflected the light back across the sand with the dull sheen of mirrors. I walked to the far side of the stadium and sat in the front row opposite the visitors' box.

The curve of banked seats extended on both sides of me, then swung in a great arc to meet the curve opposite. The high sides of the stadium sheltered its interior from cooling breezes and raised the temperature on the stadium floor. I sat there beneath the burning ceiling of the sky and watched the eddies of hot air rise from the sand. The heat seemed to increase the silence of the place. A long time before, I knew, political leaders had held rallies here, and the place had been filled with the chants of their supporters. Since then, these leaders had reappeared at the same venue, but this time their performance had been from the arena floor, and the audience judging their efforts did so from the positions that the leaders had once occupied, high up in the galleries.

The atmosphere of the place, the weight of its history, became suddenly claustrophobic to me and I got up and walked back across the sand towards the house.

3

Our keeper was in the bathroom, masturbating into a sock. He worked on himself with regular, unhurried movements, as though his mind was half on other things. I said that I wanted seedlings in the garden staked that afternoon but he did not look up or pause in his activity. In the bedroom Jan's breathing was quieter and more even now and I took the damp cloth and touched it to her eyelids, which were a faint purple, as though bruised. Her forehead still felt hot to the touch and there were spots of high colour in her cheeks.

On the wall of the bedroom, immediately above the bed, was a picture of a young woman standing in what appeared to be a swamp. A piece of red cloth was slung around her hips and her hair was piled up on her head. On her shoulder she carried a jug, which I imagined contained water. She might have been from Brazil or perhaps Indonesia, and her teeth were perfect and very white. She looked out of the painting with an open, unconvincing smile. I had seen this picture very rarely on walls in my childhood, but more frequently since then. I was interested in the woman's expression, which was not the sort of expression that you associated with swamps.

Jan woke up with a start, got up on one elbow and looked at me with with an angry, piercing look. A strand of wet hair coiled against her neck. She said something unintelligible that sounded as though it was an accusation. Something about 'talking before I could walk'. I tried to get her to repeat what she had said but she laughed abruptly and lay back on the pillow, as though she was enjoying some private joke. Shortly after this she went back to sleep. I picked up one of our keeper's magazines and started to turn its pages. I was half seeing the print and looking without understanding at the illustrations. Part of my mind was trying to make sense of what Jan had just said to me.

I thought of an autumn morning on a road leading out of an empty country town. A girl had come up behind me and touched me on the shoulder with a stick. She had jet-black hair and looked at me with a quizzical expression that I learnt with time meant nothing at all. We walked together for several hours, without talking, listening to the wires sing of the surrounding swamps. Despite the time of year the wind was warm, and carried on it the black smells of the nearby river. We came to a railway crossing where men had once died in a derailing, and I stopped and said that this was as far as I went. I intended to catch a train, I said. She told me then that she knew my destination better than I did. It was in my interests, she said, that she become my guide. I looked at her odd-coloured eyes and laughed and asked her whether she minded the smell of sulphur. For two days our wagon crossed dull farmland then veered east towards the mountains. We endured the night of an endless tunnel before emerging to the livid blue of the Pacific in an arc to the east. In the foothills of the coastal range, as the wagons wound towards the sea, we became awkward lovers on a bed of acrid yellow crystals.

After that we travelled down the coast, we stayed under bridges and in tramping huts in the foothills, although it became clear that Jan was as new to the area as I was myself. I discovered that my new lover felt no shame at this, and explained her falsehood as a partial truth that was on its way to being fulfilled. Although the fording point of a river or the layout of a town was as unfamiliar to her as it was to me, she told me things about their pasts, their significance, that she recounted hesitantly, as though recalling something from a dream. When I questioned her on the source of her information she smiled and shook her head, as though it was as much a mystery to her as it was to me.

She lay now in the damp bed, an arm back crookedly behind her head, and her hair plastered against her temples. I got up and went out into the kitchen. The caretaker was no longer in the house, and when I looked in the garden he was not there either. I skirted the garden and searched amongst the banana palms, where he sometimes rested in the shade. There was no sign of him. I walked quickly to the stadium and searched the areas that we had access to, but I felt certain that he was not there. I ran back towards the house, picked up the chain that I had used to tether him, and set off down the drive, certain now that he had attempted to escape and that he was making for a Guest suburb.

At the bottom of the drive lay a loop of road that connected with a main route beyond. Scuff marks in the dust to the right suggested the imprint of a crutch. More cautious now, I walked past the vacant lots and fenced warehouses that lined the street. I had rarely seen activity at these warehouses, and then only at night, when I had watched long vehicles, festooned with lights, unloading their contents, the crews silent and economical in their movements. We had come upon them during our early expeditions for food. The men had not looked up as we went by, as though engaged in a task that required their utter concentration.

Now I passed a chained animal that watched from behind a fence until I was almost out of sight, then broke into a paroxysm of barking. Further on I came upon a vehicle propped up off the road, its wheels removed and the glass in its windscreen missing. The street carried a faint smell of burning tyres and its surface was pitted with holes. Posters, faded with the sun, hung on walls and on warehouse doors, announcing events that had long since passed, and in some cases, events that had never taken place. I came to a part of the street where it widened before meeting the main road. I was certain that the caretaker could not have got much further, he was still very slow on his crutches and I knew his period of convalescence had left him breathless and out of condition. Although I sensed that he was near, I would have missed him if I had not seen the foot of a crutch sticking out from a pile of cardboard boxes.

He had collapsed in a narrow alley between warehouses and lay face down and immobile. I touched his ribs with the toe of my boot. He made no movement, and I was about to squat beside him when he turned over and lashed at me with his crutch. I stepped back and left him until his anger had subsided, and then I took the weapon off him while I secured the fine chain about his neck. In this way I was able to ensure that he could still use his crutches. On the route back to the stadium we passed the dog, which came close to the fence and watched us go by without any sound, as though the scene was recognisable to it now and no longer caused it alarm.

Jan had got up from her bed and sat on the veranda wrapped in a dressing-gown that was too large for her. She shivered in the dusk air as our little procession came up the drive and stopped at the bottom of the steps. She was eating cold food from a can. Her hair was pushed back from her face and her skin was waxy in the late afternoon light. She said that her appetite had returned and she was ravenous. She had woken up drenched in sweat but with a clear head. Her body still ached but she felt better than she had for days, the fever had gone. She motioned to our captive.

'Are you exercising him?'

'He went absent without leave,' I said.

'How far did he get?'

'Almost to the main road.' The caretaker adjusted his crutches, shifting his weight from his injured ankle. My lover looked down at him from the veranda. She banged the side of the can with her spoon, silencing an imaginary court.

'This is a serious charge,' she said. 'How do you plead?' He

33

loosened the chain at his neck, cleared his throat and looked towards the city. My lover stood up and pulled the dressing-gown around her. 'Sentenced to five nights in the garden,' she said, and went inside the house.

The dry period was now over, and the sudden, violent showers of late summer had begun. The air was close, and sometimes the humidity was so great that we were paralysed and sat without talking on the veranda, the perspiration running on our limbs. We no longer needed to irrigate the garden and the young seedlings grew furiously. The melon vines spread across the earth and into the palms, and we watched their growth for hours, hypnotised by this new responsibility we had for the life of the garden.

We relented over the caretaker's punishment, and after a night in the garden I brought him indoors again. When it rained he sat at the kitchen table carving wooden figurines with a penknife. The carvings were of both animals and humans, and to my surprise the caretaker was talented at his hobby. He worked with clean, angular cuts of the knife, and the creatures had a startling life to them. He placed them along the window-sill in the kitchen and on the mantelpiece in the living room, so that with time they began to form a colony of their own within the house. He used a straw-coloured wood that I had not seen before and which he polished to the smoothest of finishes. When the carving was complete he rubbed oil into the surface. The creatures were disfigured, however, by a feature that was common to them all and which the carver created with mechanical predictability. In each case the face of the carving showed an expression of the deepest terror.

Two days before the Guests were due, a tropical storm broke over the city, drumming on the iron roof with a violence that made talk impossible. We were caught inside while the wind whipped through the banana palms in the garden and our crops disappeared beneath a shallow lake of rain-water. I worried about the young plants, and after a few hours I went out into the deluge and began to excavate drainage ditches with a spade. As fast as I dug they filled with water and I stood in the rain while the water crept up to the base of the veranda and began to cover the steps of the house. Further work was futile so I went inside and watched as the storm tore away half of the palms, and the level of water grew higher. The roof sprung leaks over several of the rooms and we placed saucepans on the floor and listened to the bitter tapping of water on aluminium. Our keeper appeared unconcerned by all this, and continued with his carving as though the scene was commonplace.

After an hour or so he looked up and spoke.

'The water never comes beyond the third step,' he said. 'And in the morning the garden will be covered in new silt.' This was the first time he had spoken of his own accord. 'Without this flooding, nothing would grow here,' he continued. He completed the animal he was carving with a deft movement of the knife.

I said, 'The soil looks rich enough.' He shook his head.

'Around the stadium the soil is dead.' He paused. 'In some weathers the soil here grates.'

'Grates?'

He nodded. Jan came over and leant against the kitchen table.

'What are you talking about?' she said. The caretaker shrugged, as though offended, and took a fresh block of wood from the box beside him. He sharpened the blade of his knife on his oilstone and began a new carving. He did not look up from his work or speak again until the storm was over.

In the morning I went outside and found that the caretaker had been correct. A layer of pale silt stretched across the garden, washed down from the higher ground beyond the stadium. I removed the fine material from around the bent seedlings and re-staked them. After the rain the air was very clear, and the volcanic plugs that hunched along the skyline of the city stood out in the hard light. I walked to the stadium and inspected the sand, which had been washed a little cleaner by the rain. Water stood in long pools at various points around the arena. The rain had released the odours of past seasons from the sand and they lay in a blanket over the interior of the stadium. I put a handkerchief to my face and turned away.

The day of the visit I took the caretaker to our old home beneath the stadium. I chained him to a beam and left him with some water, his blocks of wood and his knife. Jan and I removed our possessions from the house and stored them beneath the grandstand. A little of our keeper's home-made cider remained in the wash-house. I splashed some of the liquor on the carpet in each room, and left the half-empty bottle on the kitchen table. We went through the caretaker's cupboards, removed his clothes and left them in piles throughout the house. In the kitchen I turned over the refuse bucket and scattered vegetable peelings in the corners of the room. When we had completed the impression of an employee who had slipped into drunken carelessness, I pinned to the door a note containing a rambling apology for absence, and referring to a trip to the city to obtain supplies.

We locked the house and took up a position beneath the stand with a view of the front veranda. Jan was certain that the Guests would be taken in by our deception. I was less sure. If the Guests knew our keeper at all well, they would be aware of the unlikelihood of such a decline. We watched all day, but by dusk there was no sign of an arrival. We were discussing whether to return to the house to sleep when a small boy on a bicycle appeared on the drive.

He was dark, but his hair was dyed a yellow-blond which gave him an odd, other-worldly look. On his back he carried a bag made of vivid orange plastic. Across this bag, printed in large black letters, was the slogan 'Youth First'. When he came to the veranda he got off his bike and took an envelope from his bag. He knocked, waited, then slipped the envelope under the door.

When the boy had disappeared down the drive I retrieved the envelope. A note, neatly typed and addressed to our keeper, informed him that due to commitments elsewhere, representatives of the inspectorate of recreation would be visiting the stadium a day later than planned.

To be safe we spent the night beneath the grandstand with our keeper. In the early hours of the morning I woke to a cry and a hand on my arm like a claw. Jan lay very still beside me. She had dreamt, she said, that the Guests had come straight to the stadium without stopping at the house and had begun to peel away the tiers of seats that hid us. Although this had taken them some time we did not try to escape because of our conviction that we were perfectly concealed. When finally they removed the layer above our heads and exposed us to daylight, they stood on the lip of the stand and looked down at us without surprise. One of the Guests carried a thin, chrome instrument that tapered to a point at one end and was indistinguishable from his hand at the other. Jan had no memory of the man stepping down beside her, but a short time later she felt the sensation of cold metal against her thigh. At the same moment, her dream was filled with the cloying scent of roses.

I stroked her head and watched the white line of her throat in the darkness. For the rest of the night we lay awake, listening to the whisper of cicadas in the great quiet of the stadium.

In the morning Jan did not want to discuss her dream. We slipped into a long silence and watched the drive for hours as we had watched from beneath the stadium so many times before. Again by midday there had been no sign of our visitors. There was little movement of air beneath the stand and we were bathed in a sweat that clung to our skin and soaked our clothes. In the early afternoon we made love in an aimless way, but could find no interest in each other's bodies and broke off before we had finished. We lay on our backs, dull with lack of sleep, and listened to the scraping of steel on wood from the other end of the stadium as our keeper completed another in his endless series of figurines.

I thought of the growing collection of carvings in the house, the ranks of them lined up along the mantelpiece, and the smell of the oil the caretaker used to polish the wood. I wondered absently why there had been no carvings in the house when we first arrived there in mid-summer.

We must have drifted into sleep because later I became aware of sing-song voices very near to where we lay. I got up on an elbow and looked between the cracks of the grandstand. A long vehicle, empty of its passengers, sat in the driveway beside the veranda. Its occupants were invisible from where I lay, and the sound of their voices receded a little now, as they moved in the direction of the main stadium entrance. The caretaker's incessant scratching had stopped. A little while later the visitors entered the arena, and their voices drew closer and I could hear the scuff of their feet in the sand. By moving our position a few metres we were able to see into the stadium. Beneath the ministerial box stood three men, one of whom appeared to be pointing in our direction. With time I saw that the palm of his outstretched hand was open however, as though indicating to his colleagues the scale of the structure around them. My lover was close beside me and she said something to me in a hoarse whisper that I did not catch. Then she moved away and the hot, acidic scent of her urine filled the enclosed space.

The men crossed the arena with smooth, confident movements. One member of the trio carried an aluminium case with a broad strap which he wore across his shoulder. They walked around the perimeter of the arena and stopped at the tide mark of clean sand. They stood together for several minutes and one produced a heavy book and began to examine its pages. This man had short blond hair and appeared to be the senior member of the party, and although I could not hear what he said, it was clear that he was speaking at some length to the others. After a circuit of the stadium, the group split up, and two of the men walked from the centre to the edge of the arena. One came very near to where we watched. He was so close that we could see the pitted surface of the aluminium case he carried.

At a word from their superior, the two men converged on the centre of the arena. Shortly before they met they turned abruptly on their heels and walked a diagonal back to the edge of the arena. This manoeuvre was repeated several times and each time the men walked in perfect unison, as though their steps were synchronised to a beat that was audible only to themselves. When the exercise was over, the three men made their way up into the stand in the direction of the ministerial box.

Later, much later, we heard their voices rising in volume as they passed our concealed position on their way back to their vehicle. One of them went briefly to the house, as though to check for the return of the caretaker. Then they climbed into their vehicle and drove off towards the city. When we returned to the house we stopped in surprise on the veranda. We had assumed that the Guests would have keys to the houses of their employees, but in fact the door had been neatly removed from its hinges and stood against the outside wall. The house had been thoroughly searched, but was no more untidy than before and the visitors seemed to have left everything the way they had found it.

When I finished looking around the house I found Jan standing motionless in the centre of the living-room.

'What is it?'

She pointed to the mantelpiece. Not a single carving remained. The Guests appeared to have taken the entire colony. At the centre of the mantelpiece, in place of the carvings, sat a toy that had been common at one time. These toys contained a winter landscape submerged in clear liquid, together with particles of mock snow that became a blizzard when the toy was shaken. I went to the mantelpiece. Instead of the usual landscape the sphere contained a building in perfect miniature, a structure with uneven sides that sat low and squat in the base of the globe. Around the building lay a carpet of dull flecks. If it was supposed to be snow, I thought, it was very dirty snow. I held the globe up to the light for my lover to see and the movement of liquid in the globe set the particles into a flurry of activity and in an instant the building had become invisible, submerged in a blood-red blizzard. Jan shuddered, took the toy from my hand and put it back on the mantelpiece.

'Scarlet snow. Fair exchange for his collection of horrible creatures.'

I said nothing. Instead I went to the stadium to get the caretaker. He emerged, stiff and blinking, into the daylight and I led him to the house. I took him into the living-room and pointed to the mantelpiece.

'Someone appreciates your work,' I said. Our keeper began to nod, as though the disappearance of the figures was no surprise to him, and then he backed away from the mantelpiece and sat down abruptly in a chair. He began to breathe in shallow gasps, like a panicking animal, and stood up and tried to walk from the room. He got half-way to the door without his crutches before he pitched forward onto the floor. He lay hunched in a ball, his jaw muscles working like a man bolting down food. Liquid ran in a fine stream from the corner of his mouth and collected in a pool on the boards.

Jan came out of the kitchen and stared down at him.

'Is he ill?'

I looked at the globe, where the miniature storm was subsiding and the low building emerged once more from its cloak of swirling flakes. I shook my head.

'He's failed his monthly inspection,' I said.

It was some days before the caretaker recovered from the visit of his employers. He sat in the kitchen like a man in the depths of madness, staring at his hands and talking to himself in a low, rapid voice. Occasionally he picked up a block of wood and twisted it in his hands, but his penknife remained in his pocket, and his carving ceased altogether. He would not go into the living-room and spent his nights in the kitchen, hunched up in a cane chair beside the window. Eventually I took the object from the mantelpiece and went out and buried it under the palms. After this he began to return to his former self, and I watched the colour return to his cheeks. That night, when we came to eat, he seemed to have emerged from his daze, and as he began his food he glanced at me with a careful, penetrating look that was new.

4

In the weeks that followed, I thought at times that I would be marked for ever with the scent of the arena. Through the heat of late summer I worked in the steaming heart of the place; digging and packing the sand, then taking it by trailer to the trays at the edge of the stadium where it was washed before being returned to the bed of the arena. It had been a long time since I had worked as hard, and in the first days my body was stiff with the exertion. To begin with I was hunted by the stadium's past; raw images that broke from the surface of sand like splinters of light, but I learned with time to concentrate on the rhythms of my work and push the images to the edge of my mind where they waited, unnameable shapes, for my attention to wander.

Nothing I did could rid me of the scent of the place, however, which clung to my clothes and skin and resisted my scrubbing in the tiled bathroom each night. By immersing myself in the bath I could escape the scent for a while, but as soon as I stepped from the water it was back, a faint, persistent odour, redolent of something I had smelled before but could not name.

Two days after I had buried the Guests' present beneath the palms, the caretaker approached me in the garden and said that there was something he wanted to discuss. We sat beneath the avocado and he pulled his trouser leg up to the knee. A serrated scar, like the bite of an animal, ran around his ankle. The foot looked as though it did not quite match the rest of the leg, as though it had been neatly sewn on from another body. He regarded me with his steady gaze. Although the wound had healed, the bone was now crooked, and I doubted that he would ever walk properly again.

I thought of that night amongst the palms, of the cold snap of metal, of Jan's bare legs.

'What do you want?' I said. He let his trouser leg fall.

'You mentioned an agreement. About coming to some arrangement.' I nodded. He hesitated, his face contorting, as though he had difficulty getting out the words. 'You can't be employed at a stadium without proper papers,' he went on. 'Previous employers, birth history. That sort of thing.'

'We'll pretend you're still able to do the work,' I said. 'Jan and I are just relations — refugees from the south. Beneficiaries of your great hospitality.' The caretaker nodded.

'My nephew and niece.'

'That wouldn't be much of a story, would it? How would you explain the condition of your niece?' The caretaker frowned. I wondered whether the visit from his superiors had scattered his wits.

'My nephew and his wife,' he corrected himself. 'I had one once. A married nephew that is. He used to stay here now and then. Passing through on his way south, on his way to the orchards for the harvest.'

'Is he dead?' The caretaker nodded. 'And his wife?' He nodded again.

'That's it then. New identities.'

Later, I talked to my lover about the plan. The caretaker had given me details of his nephew's life as an itinerant fruit-picker, the places he spent most of his time and the crops he was experienced at harvesting. The nephew and his wife had been childless and had followed the harvests through the northern island. His wife was foreign, from white Melanesia. 'So you're an alien from now on,' I said to my lover.

She sat on our keeper's bed, her knees drawn up under her chin. She was frowning and only half listening. She ran a hand

43

through her hair, and lay back on the bed. The woman on the wall looked down at us, the water jug poised on her shoulder. I placed my hand on my lover's belly.

'How is it?' Her eyes were fixed on the ceiling, which was discoloured in patches where the roof had leaked during the storm. Light from the window fell on her neck. Jan spoke to the patches of brown above.

'Restless. She won't lie still.'

'She?' My lover nodded. I wondered how long she had known the sex of the creature. 'Perhaps she wants some music.' Jan shook her head.

'It's too late for that,' she said and looked at me in surprise. She was back in the room then, as surely as she had been in some distant landscape only moments before.

'She's too old now,' she went on. 'She's tired of being carried around, of having tunes played to her. She wants to be out here running things.'

And in that moment I saw a child with eyes of startling green. She stood at the heart of the arena and regarded me with a deep, steady gaze, without blinking, as though watching the moment of her own birth. In her hand she held a toy, a carving made of straw-coloured wood, and beside her, his head bowed like a captive, stood our keeper. One hand hung by his side, the other obscured his eyes and he wept as though he had lost everything in the world.

Faintly, from a distance, I heard strains of music, as if a military band played beyond the walls of the stadium . . . and then I saw that the child held a glistening blade where she had once gripped the wooden toy. She turned to the weeping man, and in a ritual movement that was free of aggression, struck him in the side with the weapon, and then again until he stumbled on his feet with the impact of the blade. And now the caretaker too looked up and out from the centre of the arena and in his eyes I saw the hideous burden of his past and the dark material within him welled to his lips as a flower of blood.

44

On the bed, Jan screamed and put her hands to her belly. I walked to the corner of the room and placed my head against the wall, waiting for the image of the murderous child to fade, but it persevered like a scar on the surface of my brain. At the bed, Jan pulled off her dress as though suffocating and fell back against the pillows. I lay beside her. She was quiet now and breathing deeply. The image of the child faded and was replaced by an expanse of sand, a desert without limits or horizon. I pressed between Jan's thighs and she sighed and guided me into her body with slippery urgent fingers.

Later we sat on the bed and ate the first of our autumn melons which I had harvested that day, and watched through the bedroom window as the skyline over the city darkened. The fruit was watery and had yet to develop its full flavour, it had been harvested too early, but the cool flesh refreshed me and washed the sourness of sleep from my mouth. Although the melon was not a pure strain it was related to the commercial varieties that grew in the vast orchards beyond the city, and the euphoria crept over us slowly and we talked into the night of the seamless deception we would practise on the Guests when they next visited the stadium, and in the exhilaration brought on by the fruit we spoke of our plans for the future, something that we had rarely done before.

We took on the roles of our keeper's nephew and his wife, experimenting with new voices and postures, the mannerisms we thought appropriate to itinerant fruit-pickers. My lover practised the accent of white Melanesia, the lilting intonation and rapid delivery, and I laughed and told her that she made a frighteningly true Caldoche.

'Are you sure you don't have some of their blood, way back?' I said.

She put out her tongue and grinned. 'Let me show you how they dance,' she said. She slipped off the bed and raised her hands in invitation. She led me through a complicated series of steps that she said she had learned as a girl, and in the grip of mild intoxication from the fruit I picked up the movements without difficulty. Then we were moving lightly across the floor of the room as though we had always known the dance, dipping and swirling, and Jan's teeth showed white as she laughed and I caught the sweet scent of the melon on her breath and her odd-coloured eyes had never seemed more strange and beautiful. When we had collapsed breathless on the bed, I said,

'Who taught you that?'

'A Kanak servant. She had only one arm.'

'How can you be a dance teacher with one arm?'

'The arm was amputated at the elbow,' she said. 'There was still some left. Anyway, it's the feet that count.' Then she held up her hand to silence me.

From the bathroom came the sound of our keeper working on himself again, the slow rasp of his breath and the creak of the wooden floor as he rocked backwards and forwards.

I said, 'You had servants as a child?' She frowned, then motioned to the common wall that separated us from the bathroom.

'I wonder what he thinks about when he's doing that.'

'You, perhaps.' My lover placed her hands on her belly and smiled.

'Or you.'

I asked her again about the servant, but she got up and went to the window. She stood there in silence, gazing out over the darkened city.

'What can you see?'

She breathed in deeply, sucking in the night air. Then she exhaled and spoke to the darkness.

'A people without a past. A city in the grip of sickness.' Next door the caretaker's breathing was harsher now, and Jan's voice rose suddenly in a shout. 'A plague of masturbating caretakers!'

The sound in the bathroom stopped.

I said, 'You've ruined his climax.' She laughed, a drunken, careless laugh.

'He nearly cut my leg off,' she said. Then she put her arms around my neck and drew me too her. 'Music,' she said. 'Play your flute!'

I went to the cupboard and took out the instrument. It felt heavy and clumsy in my hands. I began to play 'Greensleeves', improvising freely as I went along, unsure of the precise fingering for the tune. I had learned in my busking years how to turn mistakes into variations that impressed with their daring.

When I finished the tune, Jan turned from the window, her eyes a little glazed.

'Now the national anthem,' she said.

'Which one?' She raised her fist and shook it at me gently.

'Just play it.' I blew the first few notes and then stopped, my lips unable to form properly over the embouchure hole.

'Go on,' Jan commanded. I started again, a little flat at first and then reaching awkwardly for the high notes of the chorus. The pads had worn and the tune was accompanied by the hiss of escaping air. Jan had turned back to the window and was looking out into the night. As I played the final descending notes, a howl broke out in the bathroom and spread until it penetrated every room in the house. I broke off the anthem. The sound died away, and after a pause I heard it repeated as a echo in the distant stadium.

I put the instrument down carefully on a table, my hands suddenly wet with perspiration. Jan stood at the window, her eyes hooded and her expression distant. I went through to the bathroom. The sock the caretaker used for his relief lay discarded on the floor and the man himself was gone. I looked through the rest of the house, and then I took the path to the stadium.

The glow of the city, reflected in the cloud cover, cast a diffuse light over the stands, so that I could see quite clearly the tiers of seats stretching upwards on either side of me. I stood in silence at the entrance to the stadium and waited, and after a time I heard the irregular shuffle of the caretaker's gait. He was in the west stand and making slow progress up the central aisle. Eventually I saw his silhouette emerge above the ministerial box. He was high up in the stadium now and from his vantage point I knew he could see the great illuminated grid of the city as it stretched away to the river.

In the silence of the stadium I heard him cough, as though clearing his throat. Then he began to sing, and the acoustics of the stadium projected his high reedy voice outwards so that it came to me clear and hard across the sand. He sang the anthem I had just played on my flute, the words a little jumbled but recognisable nonetheless, and he sang with a strange mixture of homage and parody, as though he was being forced to perform an act he did not understand. I guessed then that our keeper was imitating something he had witnessed here at the stadium, and his voice carried beyond the lip of the stands and out over the city towards the orange-lit suburbs to the north.

In the morning, stripped to the waist, I returned to the stadium with my shovel. Although the summer was nearing its end the sun was still hot and I had to break at regular intevals and rest in the shade of the stand. The tide mark of clean sand had crept imperceptibly across the stadium floor, so that now about half of the task was complete, and I knew that as I moved through the rest of the arena, progress would appear more rapid as I approached the narrow end of the oval floor. My lover often sat in the stand now and watched me as I worked. She told me that she was my overseer and was plotting my progress on a chart in her head. She brought me iced water from our keeper's refrigerator and avocados from the tree in the garden, although in her continual hunger she often devoured them herself while I worked. When I climbed up into the stand to join her, she would touch her belly and apologise for what she had done. When she looked at me with those eyes I laughed, regardless of my own hunger, and forgave her.

And always the smell, which I carried home at night and which passed inevitably to Jan's body and which followed us everywhere, a constant reminder of the events ahead of us, and the importance of my task. At the end of a day in the stadium I would lie in the bath while Jan scrubbed me with a nail-brush until my skin burned raw with the bristles. For an hour or two after my bath we would pretend that the scent had been expunged, but then one of us would look up, and like an echo the scent would be there, a thin smell that was unmistakeable, and we knew then that during the course of the day the odour had been absorbed into my skin, and no amount of scrubbing could scour the scent from the pores of my body.

As the next visit from the Guests approached, the summer showed no sign of flagging, although it was now late March. Every few days torrential rain storms would break over the city and then just as quickly clear, leaving the arena a steaming trap in which I sweated and gasped for air. In the hour or so following a downpour I would work with a handkerchief knotted around my face, gagging with the stench, until the sun baked the steam from the sand and the scent was at last dissipated. As our keeper recovered some of his former strength I got him to work on the sluicing trays, a job that he could do sitting down, and this helped speed our progress. He sat in the shade of the stadium wall with the water jet playing on the trays before him, squinting across the waste-land surrounding the stadium to the city. According to my lover's calculations, progress had been good and we had every chance of passing the next inspection.

We had rehearsed our story with our keeper, so that we were prepared for an unscheduled visit. We taught him how to move in a way that disguised his limp, in the hope that this would convince his masters he had returned to his previous status as a model, if slightly decrepit, employee.

There had been a further delivery, a case of carnival masks made of papier mâché and painted in a variety of startling colours. The masks arrived when I was working at the stadium, and Jan watched the delivery and reported that our keeper had made a weak joke of her presence to the men who had delivered the masks, a satisfactory rehearsal of the deception we intended for the Guests.

That night we tried on the masks, and Jan demanded that I strip off my clothes and stand in the centre of the bedroom while she inspected this familiar body with its lurid new face. She walked around me in her own mask, talking to herself in a whisper, and brushed my skin with her fingertips, as though both fearful and excited at the transformation she had brought about. Then she held me lightly between her fingers and encircled my prick with her lips through the mouth of her mask, but when I could stand it no more and we fell together on the bed, our masks bumped against each other and caught around our ears, so that our passion slipped away and we lay on our backs and laughed and laughed at the stains on the ceiling until we heard the front door slam and knew that we had driven our keeper from the house with our mirth.

And in the end, it was not the visit from the Guests that formed the turning point of that summer, as I had feared, but the events that followed hard on its heels, and which should perhaps have been predictable. And in a sense, everything that happened that summer was predictable, and with time it seemed to me that when the sequence of events happened as it did, it did so with an inevitability that left me certain that somehow I had known what was going to happen all along.

In the days preceding the visit I was up at dawn and worked through until the sun disappeared behind the mountains beyond the city. As was often the case at the end of summer, the sunsets were curdled by smoke high up in the atmosphere that had come from the bush-fires on the continent a thousand miles to the west, and each night for the week before the visit the sky above the stadium was lit with a bloody glow. On one such evening, his orange plastic bag bright in the dusk, the messenger boy came up the drive on his bicycle. I was sitting on the veranda in a cane chair. This was the first contact I had had with anyone from the outside since we had arrived at the stadium. He leant his bike against the veranda and walked up the steps. He blew the wave of dyed hair out of his eyes and handed me an envelope.

'What are you doing?' he said. I shrugged and gestured to the sunset.

'Watching the show. Isn't it beautiful?' He screwed up his face. He looked about eight years old.

'Foreigners,' he said. 'Polluting our fucking atmosphere.'

'What's a bit of smoke, twenty kilometres up?' He grunted and squinted into the sunset.

Then he said, 'Anyway, they've got some for the Games.'

'Some what?'

'Some foreigners. Abos.'

'Where are they keeping them?'

'I dunno. Locked up I suppose.' He had lost interest in the conversation and was walking off down the steps. I had an urge to puncture his confidence.

'The Ghost looks after his Host,' I called after him. He looked back over his shoulder, his eyes narrowed.

'Yeah,' he said. Then, 'See you later.' I watched him ride away down the drive. Jan now stood in the doorway.

'Why did you say that?' she said. I shrugged.

'He's too young to get the joke.'

'Don't you believe it,' she said.

I opened the envelope and, in the same neat typescript, a message informed us that events would proceed as scheduled, but on this occasion the caretaker would kindly ensure that he was present to accompany his employers on their inspection. I showed the note to our keeper, who nodded, tugged at his ear-lobe and said nothing.

The morning of the inspection was clear and warm, and after a last rehearsal with the caretaker, Jan and I went to the bedroom while our keeper prepared to greet the Guests in the kitchen. To complete the picture of a woman vulnerable and close to giving birth, Jan got into the bed and pulled up the coverlet around her waist. Half-way through the morning we heard the crunch of gravel in the drive, and from the bedroom window I watched a silver vehicle draw up by the veranda. Three men got out. I recognised one of them from the previous visit, the blond-haired leader, who now led his two companions to the door.

I returned to my armchair by the bed, and we listened to the rise and fall of conversation in the next room. At times the caretaker's voice seemed to crack with the stress of his explanation: he spoke of a debilitating illness from which he had now fully recovered, and assured his employers that time lost on the cleaning of this prestigious venue had now been almost entirely made up. On cue he insisted that they meet his nephew and pregnant wife, who were passing through on the way to the harvests, and who would vouch for his complete return to good health.

There was a silence, and the blond-haired man stood in the doorway to our room. He was dressed in a lightweight suit. He glanced at the dingy furnishing and his eyes went up to the stained ceiling. He stood there a while, his face expressionless, his hand on the door handle. And then with his smooth confident walk, the Guest crossed the room and sat down on the edge of my lover's bed. He looked at her swollen belly, then gently rolled back the coverlet. I found my breathing slowing, as though a paralysis had come over my lungs. I could not have spoken if I had been asked a question. The Guest drew up my lover's shirt and exposed her belly, which looked suddenly pale in the light of the bedroom. He placed a hand very carefully on her stomach and regarded her with his clear blue eyes.

'The new generation,' he said simply, and smiled. I saw then how good-looking he was, how tanned his face and manicured his hands. Involuntarily my eyes rose to the woman above the bed, to her breasts and the shout of red cloth at her waist, and I saw there the same smile and even teeth . . . aware now of the hands that stroked my lover's body, and a cry of rage was forming on my lips . . . but then the Guest was smoothing the coverlet around my lover and touching her cheek with the back of his hand. He got up and walked from the room without looking behind him. It seemed that his colleagues had been inspecting the stadium in his absence, because a few minutes later I heard the slam of car doors, and the sound of the engine in the driveway.

Shortly afterwards Jan's labour commenced, and by midnight I was certain she would not survive the night.

5

Blood and then more blood, welling between the sheets, thick, dark and warm and coating my hands and face and clothes with its terrible scent. To begin with I told her how to breathe as we had agreed I would, and to squeeze with the exhalations of air, but with time, as her agony grew and the creature would not be born, I began to lose her to another world of pain and madness. I stood at her head and whispered that the child would come in the end; I talked of marathon labours and miraculous deliveries; I spoke of the cunning of the womb, of nature's ingenious plan, of a million faultless births; and then, although I was certain she no longer heard me, I talked of our first weeks together, of the sulphur train and the darkness beneath the coastal range, of the howl of the engine, the smell of diesel, and the incandescent burst of light that brought us to the Pacific. But I had lost her now, I could no longer penetrate her pain, and I began to realise then that there was nothing I could do, and yet if I did nothing she would die.

I shouted, sang and wept; I went to the window and smashed each pane of glass in a room that now entombed us; at one point, beside myself with the horror of it all, I tore my flute from the cupboard and played her tunes that I had never heard, tunes that bore emotions that no music should be asked to bear, my fingers sticky with the dark liquid, and slipping and skidding on the keys. I stood on a drab plain amongst high poles from which hung the bodies of executed men. I knelt at the edge of a black sea in which the rotting forms of mermaids washed in the surf. I moved among these worlds in the knowledge that I was capable that night of entering one of them forever, and that only with the flute could I retrieve myself from these terminal landscapes, and only through the tunes I made up could I compose myself again in that small room. And at the height of the terror I turned and the caretaker stood there with his knife and his gold stud and his empty expression and spread his hands, and after that I felt the air turn thin and dark and the instrument fell to the floor. From the edge of a dimming circle I watched as my keeper bent over the screaming woman who was trying to give birth.

Later, much later, the pool of light enlarged in the darkness of my nightmare to include a room now lit by a humid dawn. Our keeper sat in a chair at the foot of the bed. I got to my feet and walked slowly across the room. The caretaker watched me as I approached, his face drawn with exhaustion. I stood beside the bed and looked down to where steam rose from a bowl of water on the bedside table, and mother and child lay asleep between freshly laid sheets.

The time that followed I think of as flat and grey. After a few days with my lover and her child, I went back to the stadium and worked on the sand with a steady, tireless strength. My new stamina came from having witnessed the unthinkable, but I moved now like an automaton and had to force myself to stop and eat. The food tasted of iron and lay undigested in my stomach. When I rested, which was infrequently, I watched the clouds in the oval of blue that formed the roof of the stadium, but they had lost their substance and seemed distant and two-dimensional. Everything about the stadium and our life there appeared different now, as though during the course of that night I had taken a step sideways into a world that had been bleached of its colour, and the rare and unusual had been infected with a new drabness.

The child — our child — lay with its mother in the bed, immobile, silent, and ravenous.

For days after the birth, my lover could not bring herself to speak, and when at last she did, it was in a dry, light voice and she asked for food. The child showed itself to be even more hungry outside the womb than it had been within and our keeper was sent to buy food in the markets. He brought back fish and eggs, foods we had rarely been able to obtain in the days when we had been unsure of the caretaker's loyalty. He was often away for many hours on these trips for provisions, and to begin with I questioned him on this, but he explained it in terms of his limp, and the difficulty in finding high-quality merchandise in this part of the city.

The Guests, it seemed, had been placated by the sudden progress on the stadium, although they had given the caretaker only provisional approval on their inspection, as the cleaning was still some way behind schedule. They had taken away another batch of his carvings, and had left a list of instructions for our keeper, and told him of impending deliveries, which included a boxing ring which was to become a permanent feature of the stadium.

We did not speak of the birth, my lover and I, there seemed nothing that could be said of any purpose. And somehow the child in the bed was further inhibition, as if its silent presence was a warning against discussion of the manner in which it had come into the world. Although it made no sound, it made clear its hunger very early, and gradually, over the course of the first week or so, our life in our keeper's house became oriented to feeding that one ravenous mouth, and even the task of cleaning the stadium seemed to shrink in significance beside the demands of this new-born creature. Now that the caretaker's bonus had been reinstated, we were able to buy much of what we required. Without this income I would have had to spend entire nights scavenging for food, and work on the stadium would have come to a halt.

As for the child, its presence was associated in my mind with the night of its birth, and I could not separate my feelings for the creature from the memory of those bloody sheets onto which it had tumbled so silently. I stood by the bed and watched it there, its black lashes and perfect oval face, and it lay so still that it could have been made of wax. My lover fed the creature without complaint, although I could tell that it left her sore and exhausted. Her nipples had become red and enlarged, and yet the creature would not relent. It lay on her breast, its eyes unblinking and fixed on the sky beyond the bedroom window, as if its focus of attention had been determined at birth, and it was unwilling or unable to stray from that gently varying square of blue.

Similarly we did not discuss the intervention of the caretaker on the night of the birth. I did not know what my lover thought of this, and somehow it was no longer possible to ask. While I worked in the stadium I considered our keeper's polished knife. I thought of the figurines that had sprung from its blade by day, of smooth cuts in flesh and the living child that had sprung from its blade that night. I thought of the caretaker's hours spent crouched by the bath, the seed that he spilled on the floor, and it occurred to me then that the distance in the man might in part be the solitude of the frustrated father. He continued to come and go as was his habit, and now that he was indispensable in the quest for food, I no longer put him to work with me in the stadium, I left him to his own devices.

One day he came home from the market in a new pair of trousers, the bottom half of a well-cut suit, and avoided me for some time after his arrival. It was clear that he was concerned about my reaction to his purchase, and when I met him later in the kitchen he would not look at me and immediately took up his carving. I watched him for a time, observing the sure movements of his fingers and the speed with which the completed figure emerged from the wood.

'How much did you pay for them?' I said eventually. He continued with his work, glancing down at the trousers.

'Is that your business?'

'Yes.'

'They were cheap. A widow at the market — she sells clothes from an unlicensed stall.'

'Her husband's?' I asked. The caretaker nodded. 'Where would we be without the dead?' I murmured. He put down his carving and retrieved something from a plastic bag on the floor. It was a metal coffee jug painted a bright yellow.

'She also sold me this. For three dollars.'

'What about the coffee?'

'She said she could get me some,' he said. I laughed in disbelief.

'Real coffee?' He nodded, and for a moment became animated. 'Brazilian. Strong roast and fine ground.'

'Who is this woman?'

'I told you. She's on the bottom floor of the southern market. Today she had the pot and the trousers. Tomorrow she'll have the coffee.'

'So you bought her entire stock,' I said. The caretaker went back to his carving. It was one of the longest conversations I had had with him, and as though regretting his outburst he did not speak again for the rest of the day. Later that week when the coffee failed to materialise I asked about his widow. The caretaker replied tersely that she had not shown up. For a time the coffee pot sat on the kitchen table, then one evening I saw the caretaker with a spade, and I watched from the window as he buried his useless purchase in the garden.

As though affected by the silence of her offspring, my lover began to speak less frequently herself. Her days were spent with the creature, satisfying its continual appetite, and her nights, when it no longer fed, she spent in the deepest of silent sleeps, face down in the bed with the creature between her and the wall, one arm outstretched and her fingers splayed, as though in search of an escape from a cell that had begun to imprison her. After the

58

second week, during which she occasionally got up and walked about the house with the lightest of treads, she returned to the bed, she no longer seemed to have the strength to leave it or her child. I slept, myself, in the dining-room now and as time passed I ventured into the bedroom less and less.

Our child was a girl, and well-formed, I had confirmed that on the morning after the birth. I had picked her from the bed, held her in my arms and looked into her eyes which were open and very clear. There was nothing of the squint and lolling gaze of the new-born, already she was interested in the outside, and sought out the sky above the stadium as she lay there against my chest. At one point she put out a hand and pushed my chin aside, as though my head had obscured her view of the world that was waiting for her beyond that bedroom window.

My work in the stadium had brought us close to the original schedule, and in the mornings I was now able to begin construction of the kennels that had been requested by the Guests. I made them up out of sawn beams and sheets of rough ply, a dozen or so along one wall of the stadium, and faced each kennel with heavy netting. Most river dogs were emaciated animals, with insufficient strength to escape a kennel, however flimsy, but some animals from the lower stretches of the river had access to the garbage of the Guest suburbs and were powerful creatures. I had heard the occasional story of a river dog attacking a white, but they were the wild descendants of race-bred strains, and almost always chose their victims from the population of the slums to the south.

I asked the caretaker about the arrival of the dogs, and he thought that they would be brought to the stadium a week or so before the games for training.

'Training for what?' I said. 'They don't need training.'

He shrugged. 'You know what the masters are like. They enjoy their preparations — even the unnecessary ones. It's all part of the ritual, isn't it?'

I paused. 'How many Games have you seen here?' I said. But the caretaker gazed over my shoulder and did not answer.

That evening Jan called to me from her bed. I went to the doorway and looked into the dim room. The child appeared to be asleep, and Jan was bent forward, her hands clasped at her knee. In her dry voice she asked for the trap in which we had snared our keeper.

'The trap?' I said. She nodded and leant forward further in the bed. There was a brittleness to her now, which matched the change in her voice. I sat beside her on the bed and realised then how long it had been since we had touched. I looked down at the child, its hair black against the sheets.

'Why do you want the trap?' I asked. She stared at her clenched hands, and said nothing. I shrugged, got up and went out to the shed. The trap had sat there in a cupboard since the night that my lover had acquired her new boots.

It was heavier than I remembered, and larger, as though it had been designed all along with men, rather than animals, in mind. The caretaker got to his feet as I walked into the kitchen, and his leg jerked involuntarily when he saw what I carried. I went through to the bedroom where Jan lay propped up on pillows. I put the trap on the floor under the window. I felt light-headed. I did not know whether to laugh or to protest at my lover's request.

'Do you want me to set it?' I said.

'Just leave it there,' she replied. She gazed at the trap, intently, as though seeing it for the first time, or trying to memorise its precise shape. Patches of rust had formed on the dull metal. The child lay awkwardly in the crook of her mother's arm, its limbs stiff and unsupple. It appeared also to examine the trap, to find at last in its field of vision some object of greater interest than the window onto the outside world. Jan continued to fix on the trap with eyes that were bright and hard, until I could watch no longer and went out of the room.

In the kitchen the caretaker was still standing by the table, one hand in the pocket of his new trousers. I could see his fist clench and unclench with agitation.

'What are you doing with *that*?' he said.

'I don't know,' I said. 'Maybe the child wants to see how close it came to never being born.'

I returned to my work in the stadium, to the completion of the cages and the final stages of the cleaning. My lover had retreated now, she had withdrawn into the closed circle that contained her child and the bed, and the only exit she seemed to have from this circle was through the doorway of her dreams. Often I would hear her tossing in the bed, and talking to herself in monologues of fractured poetry — rhymes and chants from her childhood years — as if she was conjuring up those distant times as an amulet against the present. Then one night I woke to a shout from her room and I went through to find her sitting upright in the bed and staring at the trap, which she had insisted I leave beneath the window. When I turned on the light I saw that a pile of food sat within the closed mechanism of the device, as though in offering. I recognised provisions the caretaker had collected during his recent trips to the markets. With one arm my lover clasped the child against her body. The other was outstretched and pointing to the trap.

'It must be fed,' she shouted. I went to the bed and sat beside her. I looked at the food that lay within the jaws of the trap.

'It is being fed,' I said.

'It's not. It won't eat.' She looked up at me with wild eyes.

'It will eat with time,' I said. 'Give it time.' Her voice was shaking.

'It won't eat. I've given it time.'

'Of course it will eat,' I said, desperate now. 'And if it's not satisfied, we'll feed it the caretaker.' She shrank away then, her back against the wall.

'Not him.' Her voice was a whisper. The child looked up at me with its clear implacable eyes.

'You must go to sleep,' I said. 'I'll look after this.' I went to the trap and picked it up off the floor. I carried it from the room and went back to my lover in the bed. I found myself speaking to the child.

'She has to sleep. She must sleep.' Jan had slipped down in the bed and lay back against the pillows. In a while her breathing slowed and she closed her eyes. I looked again at the child.

'Thank you,' I whispered, and turned out the light.

My lover craved fresh fruit now, the strange hungers of her pregnancy had returned, but according to the caretaker there were no fruit to be had at the markets, and our own melons and avocados had been finished for several weeks. When I explained this to Jan she wept, and I told the caretaker to go further in his search. Still he returned empty-handed. There was none to be found he said, the harvests had all been sent to warehouses for export. I asked him where the nearest of these warehouses was located, and he looked at me in surprise. He indicated the industrial area beyond the stadium where I had pursued and caught him a month before. 'Most of the harvest from west of the city comes here,' he said. I recalled then the vehicles my lover and I had seen unloading at the warehouses when we had first come to the stadium, their silent crews who worked late into the night.

That evening I took a jemmy from the caretaker's shed and followed the route to the warehouse. The animal had disappeared, and on the empty lot where it had been tethered the foundations of a new structure were being laid. When I came to the warehouse I took an alley to the rear of the building, away from the powerful lights that illuminated the street. I had seen no one on my walk from the stadium, but I knew there would be regular patrols in the vicinity of the warehouses.

Steel shutters covered the few windows in the building, and although I forced the jemmy into the cracks between them I could get no purchase. I continued to circle the warehouse until I came to a drain-pipe that ran to the roof. The pipe was old and rough and I was able to grip it readily with my feet and hands. From a distance I had seen skylights on the building, and now I moved along the steep pitch of the roof towards one of these structures. The skylight was covered by a heavy mesh. I worked the jemmy under a corner and prised out the screws that secured it. Then I shattered the glass beneath the mesh, and a gust of chilled air from the interior blew against my face.

I shone a torch down into the darkness. Crates lined the walls and ran in rows along the shed. Lettering on the crates stated that they contained babaco and mangosteens, and other crates were stencilled with names I did not recognise. The scent from below was like a soup on the air — thick and sweet — and after a time I felt suffocated and moved away from the hatch. I considered the difficulties of entering the building. There was a long drop to the floor, and no certainty of a way out. The doors would be locked from the outside and perhaps also fitted with alarms. I put the mesh back over the skylight, and retraced my route along the roof-top.

In the morning I found a length of rope in the caretaker's shed. At intervals along the rope I tied thick knots, until I had improvised a ladder. I explained to our keeper what I was intending to do, and that I would be gone all night. Sunset that evening was as fiery as it had been all summer and I imagined that the bush-fires were now out of control across great areas of the distant continent. When the glow had faded over the mountains and darkness had begun to settle on the stadium, I took my ladder, a sack containing the jemmy and a bundle of files, and set out for the warehouse. Again I scaled the pipe and made my way across the roof-top, but when I came to the skylight I found that a new grill had been placed over the structure and welded in place. I realised then how foolish I had been to break the glass. The shards would have been discovered on the warehouse floor during the day. For a time I worked on the grill, but the metal was a hard alloy, and after an hour I had made little progress.

I moved along the roof to another skylight, but this too had been strengthened. I wondered what other precautions had been taken to protect the building, and whether patrols had been diverted to check the area during the night. I decided to postpone my attempt. During that time I would try to find a tool that would cut the new metal of the grills. I retraced my steps along the roof, and took a different route back to the stadium. As I neared home, I heard distant shouts and the barking of dogs, but the sounds were to the east along the river, and as I listened they faded into the night.

When I approached the house through the garden I saw that the dining-room was lit up. The silhouettes of two seated figures were thrown against the blinds. I observed the house for a time from among the palms. There were no vehicles in the driveway, so whoever was visiting the house had come on foot. It could not be Guests, who were wedded to their vehicles and never walked anywhere. Perhaps the caretaker was taking advantage of my absence to make contact with someone from the outside. I knew there were other stadiums in the city, and wondered how much the caretakers had to do with each other. I moved closer to the window and looked between the slats of the blinds. The table had been positioned in the centre of the room and was covered in a white cloth, on which a meal had been laid out. At one end sat the caretaker, and at the other sat my lover.

On a dish between the diners lay a bird, a guinea-fowl perhaps, which had been half devoured. I could see the fine slick of grease on the caretaker's lips. He was dressed in a starched white shirt with the collar buttoned close to his neck. His hands, now that they had been spared manual labour, were soft and perfectly formed, and he removed the flesh from the bones of the bird with the elegance of a surgeon.

For the first time since the Birth my lover's face had taken on colour, and her eyes were wide and very bright. She was gesturing with one hand, then stretching to reach the bird and prising the flesh loose from its bones. The diners each had a bowl of water at their elbow, into which they dipped their fingers before wiping them dry on stiff napkins. Between them sat a pair of candle-sticks and a vase containing a rose. I watched the diners for a moment in time that seemed to stretch backward to my childhood and forward to the certainty of my own death in some lost corner of our decaying city. And then I turned away from the window and walked slowly to the stadium.

For most of the night I lay in the sand of the arena and looked at the sky. Sometimes, between clouds, I saw the southern constellations, and then the moon rose above the stands and its light caught the curve of the seats and was reflected in the glass of the ministerial box. At midnight a bird began to sing high up in the stands, and broke off a short time later. A few hours before dawn I drifted into a black, timeless sleep.

I woke mid-morning in the shade cast by the grandstand. Above me the sky was a uniform blue. I sat up and looked across the arena. The day before I had completed the cleaning of the sand, and it gleamed now beneath the sun. There was no trace of the scent that had hung over the stadium for so many months. I examined the palms of my hands, which were scored by weeks of work with the shovel. Eventually I got up and walked down the path to the house.

The caretaker was at the kitchen table, working at his wooden figures. He lifted his head when I came in but did not stop carving.

'She's gone,' he said. I looked into his empty face.

'What do you mean?'

'She's gone, but the child is still here.' I watched the movements of the blade against wood. For a moment I considered taking the knife from his hands and cutting his throat.

'In which direction?' I said.

'Towards the city,' he said. 'At first light.' I ran down the drive to the gate. The street was empty. She had been gone for several hours, and could have taken any one of a number of routes away from the stadium. I sat down on the kerb and watched the wind blow a sheet of newspaper along the gutter. The page caught against a fence and spread out as though displayed on a stand, the headline signalling some new government initiative. I was blind to the message. Instead I saw a table, a pair of candlesticks and a vase containing a rose. And I saw the colour in my lover's cheeks and the bright fragile way she had moved her hands across the carcass of the bird, like the movements of a priestess across a sacrifice.

A gust of wind freed the newspaper from the fence and lifted it high above the street. I watched it go, a yellowing wing, as it moved away towards the slow river to the east. After a while I got up and walked back to the house.

— II —

6

Several years earlier, at the age of fifteen, I had left my home in the rambling suburbs of our subtropical city with the intention of never going back. Certain events had befallen my family during the summer of that year, and I had been travelling ever since. In the period that followed I visited, on foot, and through the unwitting hospitality of the railway network, most of the northern island of this suffering nation. I saw, for the first time, the harsh black beaches of the western coast, whose sand burnt the feet even in winter, and where savage tides could drown a man who stood a few careless moments in water only thigh deep.

I travelled the length of the river that rose on the central plateau, skirting the dams and feeding on the pink-fleshed fish that lived in the lakes below. I avoided cities and occasionally, when I needed money, I busked in the small towns of the interior. Musicians were not often seen in these places and I could assure myself of a few dollars by playing the simplest of tunes. When these townspeople stopped and spoke to me, which was rare, it was usually to ask the name of the instrument I played or request a tune they had not heard for many years. Nostalgia for a time I had never known was common in these towns, but the requests were often whispered, as though my listeners were indulging a vice of which they were ashamed.

I met other travellers, who told me of the risks of being seen in the vicinity of the orchards that covered so much of the countryside. The high fences made these places visible from a distance, however, and I had little difficulty in avoiding them. Once, after jumping from a freight train at night, I had come upon an orchard without warning, and saw beneath the floodlights what appeared to be the body of a child stretched against the netting, its hands on the upper wires, its feet shoeless and still.

Most often, during my travels, I slept rough, in moving wagons and under bridges. The stadium, in fact, was my first proper home in three years. Similarly, the relationship with my lover was my first of any length. There had been couplings with others, travellers and free gatherers of both sexes and several races, invariably in circumstances that did not encourage permanence or promises of fidelity — I speak of dank barns, burnt-out houses, the rancid shells of fallen abattoirs.

The stadium then was the first home of my own, and the mother of the child was my first real love. And however perverse this may seem, it is also true that I looked upon our keeper, in some senses, as my first father. I had never had a father, or at least could not recall him clearly, and the notion that a man could be both father and adversary was not in the least bit strange to me. In fact in these emaciated times I had met others who had told me that, more often than not, fathers were bitter enemies to their children. The possibility that my new father — the keeper — might betray or kill me (or, for that matter, I him) was a matter that was never far from my mind.

In the event, the caretaker would say nothing of the meal I had observed, or his part in the circumstances of Jan's departure, despite my threats. On the third day after she had gone, deranged by his silence and the sudden realisation of my loss, I chained him to the avocado and cut off his ear-lobe with the kitchen scissors. Still he was silent. I removed the stud and made him eat the scrap of flesh, which he swallowed with some difficulty before fainting. When I revived him with the garden hose, he still would not speak, and although I left him chained to the tree for several days so that the autumn winds might gnaw at him, eventually I set him free. He would be observed, I knew, by the truck operators making deliveries for the games.

When it became clear to me that he would not discuss the matter of the banquet, I returned his gold stud. Some time later he pierced his other ear and wore the stud then on the left.

The child grew up with unnatural rapidity. She adapted to the sudden need to eat solids, and I fed her boiled sweet potato, a vegetable that could be obtained in unlimited quantities from the markets. I cooked the tubers in a large pot on the stove, then mixed them with a little milk and fed the mush to the child with a spoon. She ate all of what she was offered, and as usual it was almost impossible to satisfy her appetite. I asked the caretaker to construct a high chair for the child, which he completed within a few days. To begin with she sat in the kitchen with us during meals, but although I fed her first she observed us eat with ravenous eyes, to the point where I could no longer dine under her gaze. After that, when she had finished her meal, I took her to her room and put her to bed. At first I tried to sleep in the same room as the child, but I found myself tossing all night on my mattress on the floor, aware of her silent shape above me in the bed. Eventually, unable to find any rest, I removed the mattress and slept next door in the living-room.

In the first weeks after my lover's disappearance I listened for the scuff of gravel on the drive. I heard her footsteps in the creak of the iron roof, in the rustle of banana palms and in the murmur of the distant city. Later, days went by when I believed I had exorcised all thought of her return, and then I would be caught by some random sound and feel the sweat break out on my palms, the twist of hope in my chest. After a month I gathered up the things she had left — a few clothes, a pack of cards, a branch of black coral — and put them back in the sandalwood box she used for her possessions. On occasion I would open the box and

71

hold a shirt against my face, but with time the scent of her faded on the cloth, and I lay awake on the mattress at night, lost in insomnia, trying to conjure up the fruit and salt of her skin.

I watched my father, and wondered how much he knew. He had taken to wearing the fine clothes he had acquired at the market, the stiff shirts and well-cut trousers, and was more particular about other matters as well. He shaved more frequently, and manicured his finger-nails, as though intent on throwing off his former role of manual labourer . . .

I finish nailing the metal plates to the floor and stand, light-headed, my hands on the ropes that bound the ring. The pale sand stretches to the main gate. I walk, my feet scuffing lightly on the surface, and although the wind is now circling the stadium and blowing a mist of sand before me, I can hear no sound, the wind is silent in its touch, a force that acts without audible trace. Above me, the glass eye of the ministerial box looks down, malevolent sensor, it has command of this place, no corner escapes its attention. In the sand-spume of the arena I see now the unnameable shapes, which I force from my mind and I walk on through silent wind ...

Each morning when I rose I buried myself in the routines of preparation, until the days acquired an equilibrium of sorts. Deliveries arrived more frequently now — banners, crates of opera-glasses, sound systems; the paraphernalia of organised spectacle. These crates were lowered from the back of large vans, then transferred to the sheds beneath the stadium on a trolley. Instructions from the inspectorate came with the equipment, much of which was to be installed at some time in the future by the Guests' own technicians. According to the caretaker, who despite his mutilation conversed with me much as before — sparingly and without emotion — these people were specialists at their job, and went from city to city throughout the country performing the same task. Most of them, he said, were women.

The river dogs were delivered about this time, and the catchers had been unsuccessful in their attempts to find decent

72

specimens. We were given five of the animals, which arrived one morning in a caged truck, silent and emaciated, little more than starving curs. With them came a freezer full of meat, and instructions for feeding. The driver informed us that a trainer would arrive in a week or so for daily sessions, by which time, he said, the animals were expected to be fattened and energetic. When the dogs had been transferred to their cages and the truck had driven away down the drive, the caretaker peered at them through the netting.

'Miracles. They expect miracles,' he said, and tugged at his ragged ear.

The next visit was by a group from the Ministry of Recreation, and occurred soon after the arrival of the dogs. There were no Guests in the party, and once the men had satisfied themselves that the cleaning of the arena was complete, they showed no further interest in us. The men spent an hour or so in the stadium, and went to the sheds where the delivery material was stored. They examined the crates and checked their contents against an inventory. When they had completed this task they left without speaking to us further.

Most days now were spent unpacking equipment and laying it out in the store-rooms beneath the stadium. Masks, it seemed, were to be widely used in the games. We had already received one case — the brightly coloured faces my lover and I had tried on. Now another shipment arrived. There were black-minstrel masks made of stiff cardboard, with exaggerated lips and gleaming, curly hair. There were clowns' faces with cherry noses and flapping ears. And there were animal heads, the kind that could be placed over the shoulders — donkeys, bears and giraffes. Although imitations, they appeared life-like, as though real skin and fur had been used in their construction.

We had laid out the heads on a table, and I suggested to my father that he try one on. He looked at me with his blank eyes and pursed his lips. He held up a donkey head. 'Don't you think it would suit you better than me?' he said.

I walk from the arena and observe the house, the warehouses, the sullen city, and to the west the line of mountains beyond which the ocean seethes and waits, reined in by the freakish hand of that western wind ... A sea-gull turns against a white sky. At the house the soundless gate slams and opens, slams and opens, a broken latch, rotting boards that scar the veranda, the front door ajar. I open the door and go inside ...

Awake with the light each dawn, I lay on my mattress and listened to the dogs. The creatures had begun to put on weight, and to paw at the wire of their cages. There were four males and a bitch, and when the latter went on heat the sound of the animals kept me from sleeping. I would lie there for hours, adrift on a sea of half-sleep, recalling the earlier times. Years before, during my travels in the far north, an animal with the brindle markings of a river dog had befriended me. She had followed at a distance through the outskirts of a town, ignoring my attempts to frighten her off. For a time I thought I had lost her, but that night, as I slept beside the concrete pier of a bridge, she came to sit beside me in the dark, and in the morning had adopted me as her own.

For weeks she followed me faithfully, a few paces behind, and I no longer had the heart to frighten the creature away. Occasionally she caught rabbits and stoats, and required no extra feeding from me. With her sharp face and small eyes, she resembled a leader who appeared frequently on the television screens I watched in shop windows, and whose name appeared to be Meringue. This man, they said, had been one of the few leaders the Guests had kept on, and although the shop window televisions were inaudible to me it was possible to tell that he was unusually stupid.

Meringue became skilled at boarding trains, and could often detect the sound of a freight train on the tracks long before I could hear it myself. The creature stayed with me for months before she was finally betrayed by her breeding. We had been travelling on a flat-decked carriage through the native forests of the north. It was September and warm, with occasional light rain that dried quickly on the skin. We passed a gang of loggers working on a site near the line, and immediately my companion's fur stood up. Before I could grab the cord around her neck Meringue had leapt from the carriage. She misjudged the speed of the train and broke her back on the rail embankment. By the time I got to her she was almost dead. I called to one of the loggers and he ended her pain with a single blow from his machete.

After that I avoided strays, and my next travelling companion was my lover.

Now, at the stadium, the river dogs were so restless and pawed at the wire with such persistence that I strengthened the cages. At first the caretaker exercised the dogs, but as they increased in weight it was clear they were becoming too much for him, and I relieved him of his task. I took the animals to the stadium and let them loose on a long cord, so that they could run in circles around the arena floor. One of the dogs had become so strong that I found him difficult to restrain, and when I took him to the stadium he would drag me across the sand, his powerful legs ploughing up the surface. Eventually I could no longer risk taking him out, and he remained in his cage, pawing furiously at the netting when the other animals were let out, and whimpering if I came near.

In the bright and sterile kitchen sits a man whom I know, who may dress well but is now clothed in the garments of a labourer, a keeper, the attendant of a human zoo. I move to him and brush his skull with my fingers (it is newly shaved, as though for devotions) and detect, although I do not look down, the efficient movements of a master carver. Through the deep silence, beyond the house, beyond the city, comes the murmur of a rising ocean. I turn away and follow the passageway of the house, until I come upon a door, beyond which waits a crazy, luminous child ...

I was woken one morning by the messenger boy rattling my window. I got up and went out to the kitchen. The note informed us that the opening of the games was to be set back a few days. The new start date, said the note, had not been determined precisely, but we would be advised as soon as this information was available. I questioned the messenger on the reasons for the delay, but as unhelpful as always, he simply shrugged and walked from the kitchen. Out on the veranda, the child sat against the wall, and as he passed her, the delivery boy stopped and squatted down. He remained there for a time, watching the child, and then he got up and climbed onto his bicycle. He hitched his orange bag over his shoulder, hesitated, and then rode away. Half-way down the drive he pulled his bicycle into a skid, and gazed up the drive. He was looking back at the child. I went to the door, and when he saw me appear on the veranda he rode off. I picked up the child. I thought then how heavy she was for her age.

The caretaker had been standing near the door. He watched me as I carried the child inside.

'He's curious,' he said. 'There aren't many children her age in this part of the city.' When I asked him why this was the case, the caretaker said that he did not know. The matter did not seem to interest him greatly. That night we discussed the postponement of the games. The caretaker said that a similar delay had occurred several years ago. For no apparent reason the opening ceremony had been put back by several weeks. The Guests never explained the delay, but the caretaker had assumed that certain participants had been unavailable at the time required. We agreed that so long as we could make the food for the river dogs last, there would be no difficulty in adapting to a later schedule.

There was little more to do apart from erecting the ring that had been requested by the Guests. The structure consisted of a number of prefabricated sections that had to be bolted together.

The caretaker avoided the heavier labour, and appeared to exaggerate his limp when asked to carry materials. After the partitions had been put in place I began to fit metal panels to the floor of the ring in accordance with the assembly instructions. I asked the caretaker the reason for these panels, and he told me that they were designed to absorb the heat from the sun.

'The performers appear in bare feet,' he said in his high voice. 'Spectators find this amusing.'

When the last of the plates had been laid I removed my shoes and walked out onto the ring. Although the sun was hidden by cloud, the metal was very hot. After a minute the heat became unbearable, and I had to run for the edge of the platform. I inspected my feet. Even in the brief time I had been in contact with the metal, a blister had formed on my heel. The caretaker had watched my experiment without expression. I asked him whether he had witnessed these spectacles, but again, in response to a direct question about his part in the games, the caretaker did not answer.

I looked up into the stand, where the child had been sitting quietly in one of the lower tiers. I had discovered early that she had a strong sense of her own safety, and it was possible to leave her alone in the grandstand, where she would amuse herself for hours. Even from this distance I could tell that her gaze was fixed on the activity below her. She had watched us construct the ring. Now she followed my father with her gaze as he left the stadium. And then she appeared to grip the seat beside her and get to her feet . . .

In the emptiness of the passage I wait, beside the darkened door, but the child does not summon me. Eventually, I knock, but she does not answer. Behind the door I hear the sound of distant laughter, the noise of children playing on the beaches of childhood, and then the trickle of water in the streams of the south. I turn and walk slowly back down the passage to the kitchen. There the keeper waits, transformed now in dress; immaculate cuffs and gleaming links, a butterfly of stiff fabric at his neck. He smiles, he brushes his lapels with supple hands, he taunts me with a rose …

The sun came out from behind a cloud and reflected violently from the sand so that for a moment I lost sight of the child. I squinted through the glare. Then the sun was eclipsed by moving cloud and I could see her again, now seated. Could she have stood?

Overcome by a father's anxiety, something that was new to me, I hurried across the arena and took the concrete steps to where she sat. She looked up, a level, serious appraisal. I reached out and touched her face. I brushed the curls away from those startling eyes, and lifted her in my arms. The sun broke through the clouds. At the head of the stadium the metal surface of the ring flashed fire into the stands.

The keeper is on his back, scattering sand, old man's spittle, and the thrashing of aging, futile limbs. He is too slight to resist, and I pin him down, he cannot flee, a participant now in the spectacle he has so meticulously prepared. The laughter of blade on flesh, and then I hold the severed hands to the sky, to the oval painted sky, to the gaze of a smoked-glass lens, behind which the modern emperor sits, invisible within his box. I have them now, the trophy that I am owed. The sound of a faceless crowd swells in the stalls around me. I stand, I bow, I weep.

7

Dreams. I had listened to my lover's descriptions of these events in the way that I listened to the people I met who had travelled abroad. I showed scepticism, half-knowing this grew from disappointment at being barred from these imperfect rehearsals for an unknowable future. And as nothing had prepared me for fatherhood, or for being a son, so nothing had prepared me for my new capacity to dream.

Now, as I began to invent myself as a father and son, I thought that my new-found skill as a dreamer might help.

One lunchtime my father walked into the kitchen and sat down at the table. I heard the sound of his knuckles crack and looked up. He watched me, his hands steepled on the table. I knew that this gesture signalled the onset of some anxiety in the man.

'There's someone living here,' he said.

'In the stadium?' He nodded. He examined the back of his hands with a fixed expression.

'How do you know?'

He gestured vaguely. 'The way I knew when you arrived. They've been here the last few days.'

'What do you want to do. Trap them?' I said. He shrugged.

'We have to do something. It's too close to the games. The Guests like their stadiums clean. Clean of filth, clean of marginals.'

That night, to test the caretaker's theory, I left some food in the arena. In the morning it was gone. I asked him what he proposed we do. He frowned.

'We could leave a note. Threaten them with a gassing. Anything. But we should do it straight away.'

I wrote out a message in block letters, explaining the danger of colonising the stadium at this time, and advising our guest that the games were to begin shortly. Again I left food in the arena, and attached the note to the cardboard box containing the provisions. The next day the food was gone, and the note and box remained. We did not put out any more food, but two days later the caretaker said that our visitor was still in residence. That evening, as I ate my meal, the caretaker came into the kitchen. He had shaved his head, as he did from time to time, and with his stubble and mutilated ear he looked like a famous painter whose likeness I had seen as a child, but whose name I had now forgotten. This painter had seen the world as a sea of writhing energy, and had eventually gone mad.

My father was carrying a sack, and now he took the trap from the sack and placed it on the table.

'It's still in working condition,' he said.

'Get out,' I said. He looked at me as though he did not understand, although I knew he understood very well. I pointed to the door. 'Get out,' I repeated. 'And take this away.' I got up from the table and flung the trap at the door. My keeper walked over, picked it up and left the room. That night I heard him experimenting with the device on the veranda late into the evening.

In the morning I was woken by the messenger boy knocking very early. He handed me the usual cream envelope. Before I had time to open it he spoke.

'They're off.'

'What are?'

'What do you think?' He could hardly stand still. 'The games. The fucking games are off.' He was reporting something he sensed was of major importance, but which he did not really understand. I ripped open the envelope.

'Why?' I said. He screwed up his face until it looked as though it might tear. I could see that he did not know the answer, and hated having to admit this.

'Dunno. Maybe you didn't fix things up properly,' he said hopefully.

'We've spent three months preparing. Everything's finished.' His face was still contorted. 'Calm down,' I said and touched his shoulder. 'It's not your fault, is it?'

To my surprise, a tear formed in the child's eye and rolled down his cheek. He snatched at it angrily.

'What is it?' I said gently. 'Do you have a season-ticket or something?' We both knew that children were barred from the games, but he was furious that I had seen him cry, and ran down the steps. He jumped on his bike and rode at breakneck speed along the drive, almost colliding with the gatepost at the bottom.

The envelope contained a note that conveyed the news in the usual bland way, without elaboration. The games had been cancelled. More details would be made available soon. I thought of the river dogs, and how we would feed them. Then I went in to my father, and shook him awake.

'The games are off,' I said. 'No games this year.' He turned over.

'You're lying.'

I waved the note at him. My father took the message, gingerly, with his fingertips. He held it to the light to check the watermark and then sat bolt upright in his bed.

'No games,' he said slowly.

Later the caretaker unearthed a hidden cache of liquor in the garden, finished off several bottles of the brew and went to the stadium to address his persecutors. When I found him he was high up in the stand, singing and shouting to the empty

81

amphitheatre. He hurled an empty bottle out into the arena, where it lay in the sand like a message-bottle on a pale sea.

He stood on the ministerial box, unsteadily, a hand outstretched for balance. To the best of his knowledge, he announced to his invisible audience, in defiance of the odds of history, for some unknown but instantly celebrated reason, they, the elect, the well-organised voyeurs of this diseased and god-forsaken city, were to be denied, for one year at least, the spectacle after which they continually lusted, the barbarous ritual which as upright citizens of a prostrate city they so predictably sought, year after year, the festivities around which his own life revolved like a dead planet in a dying solar system, the municipal ritual for which he, the caretaker and mascot of this flea-bitten venue so tirelessly prepared each season, without fail, wind, hail or flood, crippled or whole, harassed by social parasites or abandoned in his loneliness, and even if it was true that he, the toiling one, the servant of their perversion — who had once known higher office — on occasion, out of sheer frustration at the barren sameness of his life, took part in — perhaps even enjoyed — one or two of these activities, even if this was the case, he wanted them to know that he was overjoyed that in one year at least, for whatever reason, by whatever unexplained act of god or nature, they had been deprived of the pleasures they craved.

Later, when my father had fallen from the roof of the ministerial box and I had dragged him down the stairs of the stadium, he continued to talk, though in gibberish now. I got him with difficulty across the sand of the arena, and down the path to the house. Although he was a slight, wiry man, he was so drunk that he was incapable of helping himself, and several times, exhausted, I dropped him, and watched him huddle there on the ground, his lips still murmuring nonsense. Eventually I propped him in the kitchen chair where I could examine his ankle, which was swollen and bruised.

'Where did you learn to make speeches like that?' I said. He peered at me with watery eyes, and his head lolled forward. I packed ice around his ankle and left him slumped over the table to sleep off the effects of the liquor. Some time later, when he had still not moved, I carried him to his bed.

I sat on the veranda and watched the river dogs paw at the wire. The festivities were a major event in the Guests' calendar. Only something of importance could have brought about their cancellation. After a while I got up and walked over to the cages. The dogs were now too large for their enclosures. I knocked the pins out of the locks and threw open the doors. If asked, I thought, we would say we had run out of food for them. The animals loped around me in circles. Then two of them headed for the stadium and the others walked to the top of the driveway, looking back uncertainly. I waved my arms and they ran off towards the city. I followed the others to the stadium where, as though programmed by their periods of exercise, they ran around the perimeter track, following the path they had worn in previous weeks. After a while, sensing their new freedom, they broke from the track and made for the base of the grandstand, where they began to dig purposefully at the sand. I could see the fur on their backs was raised. I went for a piece of bamboo. When I returned the dogs had almost burrowed under the apron of the stand. I beat them with the stick until they ran off, their ears flattened and their fur still raised.

When the caretaker woke up he was pale and drawn and limped into the kitchen on his bad ankle. He sat down carefully at the table. The child watched him from the floor, turning one of the caretaker's half-finished figurines in her small fists. I asked my father whether he remembered his speech. He glanced at me, his eyes bloodshot.

'What did I say?'

'You announced your pleasure at the cancellation of the games. You said you weren't in favour of them, and made some critical remarks about your employers. Then you fell off the ministerial box.' The caretaker shuddered, and kneaded his hands.

At our feet, the child banged the figurine on the floor, as though wanting our attention. She already seemed many times her actual age, and appeared to grow perceptibly with each day that passed. I gestured to the child. 'Perhaps she heard you too,' I said. The child looked up at us from the floor with her steady green eyes, and it was possible in that moment to believe that she had not only heard the speech, but had understood every word of it. The caretaker put his head in his hands. 'And what else have you got buried in the garden?' I went on.

'Nothing,' he said in a muffled voice. 'That's the last of it.'

That night I dreamt that my lover and I sat in the stadium and watched our keeper give an oration to the assembled masses. At the conclusion of a speech in which he spoke of the difficulties of the caretaker's life, of impossible burdens and unreliable schedules, of the feeding needs of exotic animals and the effect on his health of all those toiling years, he took his penis in his dry surgeon's hands and began to work on himself with steady, purposeful strokes. A murmur of approval rose in the stalls around us, and swelled into a low roar that filled the stadium. One by one the audience got up to applaud the spectacle, and with time the entire stadium was caught up in a standing ovation. And then my lover was on her feet and threading her way through the crowd to our keeper. She knelt down and began to wash his genitals with a cloth and a bowl of water. At the completion of her task, she removed the boots she had stolen and placed them on the feet of their rightful owner.

I woke in a sweat in the dark, my mind struggling with the shreds of the dream, and listened to the faint snarl of my keeper's sleeping breath in the room next door.

With the termination of the games we were thrown into a limbo that lasted for months. There was no news of the reason for cancellation. The caretaker said he had asked at the market but had been unable to discover anything of substance. There were rumours circulating, he said, but none that were conclusive. It was known that the games were timed to coincide with the completion of the end-of-summer harvest, and one rumour had it that there had been a failure at the orchards. This theory was contradicted by the stream of vehicles through the industrial suburbs nearby, and the packed warehouse I had seen on my night-time visit. Another rumour suggested trouble in the slums to the south, but the caretaker said there was no evidence to support this either.

We assumed that we would be required to pack up the materials that had been supplied for the games, but neither of us wanted to begin until we had heard again from the Guests. I asked the caretaker whether it was possible to contact his employers directly and request their instructions. 'It's possible,' he said and grimaced.

Although we left out no food, we fed our unknown visitor nevertheless. Vegetables would go missing from our garden, or a can of soup left carelessly on a window-sill would disappear overnight. I began to feel that I knew our guest, and imagined him crouched in some corner of the stadium as my lover and I had done, feeding on the produce of the caretaker's garden and scavenging for provisions at night. Although the need to get rid of him had been removed by the cancellation of the games, it was clear the caretaker resented the presence of the trespasser, and I felt that there was a chance he would attempt to snare him. One morning, before the caretaker woke, I took the trap and hid it in a distant store-room.

Throughout the winter, as the child grew up, and the gap left in our lives by the cancellation of the games lengthened and deepened, the caretaker began an obsessional search for the stranger who had entered his domain. At dawn he stalked the outside perimeter of his territory, and as night fell he would often go to the stadium and take up a position in some inconspicuous corner of the stands, where he would sit for hours, huddled in a blanket, watching for the trespasser to show himself. I said that a confrontation with a younger man, a desperate free-gatherer perhaps, might lead to serious injury, but he ignored me and went on with his patrols, carrying with him now a short club which he kept in the waistband of his well-cut trousers.

The days, when not tending the garden, I spent in educating the child, whose intelligence was clear, and who listened as I read to her from our keeper's small collection of books with a concentration that was unmistakable. She had not repeated the feat of standing since the day I believed I had seen her get up in the stadium, and neither had she uttered a sound. She communicated through the directness of her gaze and the expressiveness of her small white hands, with which she gripped my arm or pointed out objects she desired. Her eyes were the most intense of colours, as beautiful as her mother's, and yet her face had a waxen immobility that conveyed the impression of someone many years older. Sometimes, when she sat there on the floor as I read to her from some dusty encyclopaedia, I had the sensation of being observed by an ageless, impassive, doll.

One afternoon I took her to the sheds beneath the stadium where the materials for the games were still laid out on the tables. Her interest was caught by the masks, and as I held her up to the table she touched them carefully with her small hands as though they were sacred objects in our temporary custody. She was less reverent with the opera-glasses, and wanted to go outside with them. I held them to her eyes so that she could look out over the city to the north and then I turned her so that she was able to view the sprawl of slums to the south, with the faint haze of dead air settled over them like fine gauze.

And in the end it was not the choleric patrols of my keeper that led to the identification of our visitor — but the cold. One morning, after a succession of clear chill days towards the end of the winter, I was woken by the child beside my mattress. She gripped my arm. We looked at each other for a time before I realised that she wanted me to get up. I went to the kitchen. On the veranda outside, his back against the wall, was a man in a woman's pale-blue negligée. He was thinner that anyone I had ever seen, and very black, and his beard was touched with a rime of frost. He lay on his side, the negligée barely covering his narrow buttocks, and did not move when I touched his shoulder. Although he was a tall man, he was so light that I had no difficulty carrying him inside. I wrapped him in a blanket, put him in a kitchen chair and ran a hot bath. When the bath was full I removed his negligée. His body was covered in lice and sores, and I noticed that the fingers on one hand had been broken, and lay at strange angles to each other. I carried him to the bath and lowered him into the water. After an hour or so his eyes opened and he looked at me dully. I dried him, wrapped him in blankets and took him to a mattress.

The caretaker had woken now, and watched me lay the man on the bed. He stared at the trespasser who had eluded him for so long.

'An Abo,' he said, in disbelief.

After two days, the trespasser was able to sip a little toheroa soup that I fed him from a spoon. I had difficulty getting the liquid into his mouth because of his constant shivering, which only stopped when he drifted into sleep. His black eyes were emotionless, and he said nothing. I had found a cream in the bathroom for his sores, and explained to him what it was for. He gave no sign that he understood, and when he took the jar in his hands I could see that he did not have the strength to unscrew the top. Eventually I unwrapped him from his blankets and applied the ointment myself. To rid him of lice I shaved his head and beard with the instrument my keeper used, and at first he resisted, but he was too weak to do so effectively, and soon gave up.

He lay on the floor of the living-room near my own mattress, and for the first week, once the shivering had gone, he was still and made no sound. Then one night he woke me with a screaming fit in which he referred to a cell, a machine for smashing hands, and the yellow teeth of predatory dogs. After that he went back to sleep and did not wake for several days. To begin with I thought he had entered a coma, but his breathing was regular and deep, and I thought it best to leave him to sleep off the terrors that pursued him.

8

When eventually he woke he ate some food and his eyes seemed sharper. He watched us come and go in the house for days, still silent, although I knew he spoke our language because of the outburst in his sleep. In case he had some attachment to the negligée, I washed it of its grime and left it by his mattress. He scratched the stubble of his missing beard.

'Take that bloody thing away,' he said. I looked at him and laughed.

'I didn't think you wore it by choice,' I said.

'All that was available,' he said. 'Not much good for a winter in this damn place. And what have you done with my beard?'

'You had some unwelcome wildlife,' I replied. He rubbed his chin with his good hand and pulled a face. He said that he had picked up the infestation at his last place of residence, an institution he referred to as the Hotel.

'Lice were encouraged for nutritional reasons,' he said. 'We couldn't breed them fast enough.'

'What kind of hotel is this?' The Aborigine showed his discoloured teeth in a smile.

'It's an odd shape, for a start. You're encouraged to stay for longer than you want.' He waved his crushed hand. 'And the service isn't very good.' He had arrived at the Hotel the year before, he said, together with a number of his countrymen. They had stayed for six months.

'The nigger wing was full up,' he said. 'Lizard clan, honey-ant, wallaby, you name it. The whole zoo. We heard a new lot was due in. They wanted us to move on somewhere else. Somewhere less luxurious.' The vehicle carrying the men had been involved in an accident, he said. They had overpowered their attendants and got away. He drew the blanket around his narrow shoulders. 'They're a bit careless with entertainment-class detainees.'

'And the others?'

He shrugged. 'Spread around the city, maybe.'

He was from a lizard dreaming clan in the northern territories of our great neighbour to the west. As an elder he had become an authority on a piece of desert the size of our own country. He had been educated by priests, and trained for a while as a novice himself. During this time he had become a world authority on the killer pope, Pius V, and the pederast Paul IV. His scholarship had been rewarded with a denunciation and expulsion from the fold. He was still able to recite the Latin Mass. 'Communions to order,' he said. 'You supply the wine.'

I told him I had never attended a church in my life. 'No worries.' He gripped my shoulder with his bony hand and smiled. 'The proselytising days are over.'

When prevented from further excavating the past of the strange rulers of his faith, he developed his skills as a star-gazer and astronomer, and that evening he got up from his mattress and took me outside to explain the sky. He rested his long arms on the veranda rail and told me of the invisible links that ran among the stars.

'That', he said, pointing to a cluster over the stadium, 'is the Centaur. Half bull, half man. He kills with an ebony bow.' As I picked out the lines of the beast in the cold clear sky, I thought suddenly of the messenger boy's comments some months before.

'Do you know why they were keeping you?' I said.

'Some circus or other. They wanted a bit of foreign colour. We weren't all that keen on the idea. The pay didn't sound too good.' We both laughed. I described my conversation with the messenger boy and told him about the games.

'You've ruined the main event of their year,' I said. 'They'll never forgive you.'

In the morning I took the Aborigine to the stadium and showed him packing cases, the masks, and the rest of the props intended for the games. He wandered out into the centre of the arena, shading his eyes from the sun. He ran his toe over the surface. 'Nice clean sand,' he muttered. Indicating the boxing ring at the end of the arena, he said, 'I watched you build that thing.' He gazed around him. 'How many does this place hold?'

'Sixty thousand.' He stroked his missing beard.

'Quite an audience.'

The caretaker agreed to part with some of his old clothes, which were too small for the lanky Aborigine. The corduroy trousers came to mid-calf and split at the crotch. He stood before the mirror in the bedroom and admired the effect. He hadn't been so well-clothed, he said, in many months. The caretaker watched us from the door. He had said little since the arrival of the black, and I knew that he was unhappy with another guest in his house. He rarely spoke to the Aborigine, replying to questions in monosyllables. He showed no open hostility, however, and had given up one of his mattresses when requested.

The Aborigine was weak from his time as a fugitive and after his months in the darkness beneath the stadium he had an aversion to sunlight. He spent his first weeks at the house with the curtains drawn. He wandered from room to room, whistling between his teeth, and occasionally stopped to unfold his long limbs in a set of the most graceful exercises. He stood like a bird on one leg, his eyes closed, and raised the other foot until it touched the inside of his thigh. Then he bent forward until his torso was parallel to the floor, extending his arms behind him like wings. These movements, he said, were to regain his suppleness after the months of confinement. At dusk each day he chanted a song which was always the same, and which filled the house with a nasal vibration.

He was interested in the child and spoke to her gravely and as an equal. I watched them together on the floor of the room, the child with her solemn face, and the black with the beginnings of his wispy, Pharaoh's beard, and he told her stories of the creation, of birds with calls like humans, of animals that were made up of the parts of other animals, and of the vast horizons of his home. Often the child appeared to be absorbed in her own world, but this did not deter him. He sometimes addressed her in his language, a tongue with an unpronounceable name, and when I asked him why he did this, he said that language had its own music that was separate from meaning, and that such music was as important to a child as the music of instruments.

Later, when he had put on some weight and rid himself of the sores that covered his body, the Aborigine went back to sleeping beneath the grandstand. He did not wish to be surprised by a visit from his captors, he said. After the evening meal each night he stopped for a time on the veranda to examine the stars. He told me that new stars were born each day and existing stars were dying, and he liked to keep his knowledge of the heavens up-to-date. The skies above his home, he said, were the clearest in the world, and it was possible to see constellations that were invisible everywhere else. During his time at the Hotel he had glimpsed the night sky through a small window high up in his room. This, he said, had saved him from disintegration. Once, towards the end of his stay, he saw a pair of shooting stars cross that black square, and he knew then that escape was simply a matter of time.

Each night, after he pointed out the slow march of some new constellation across the heavens, he walked down the steps and into the darkness.

The delivery boy had not called during the winter months. I had seen nothing of him since the day he rode away in tears, and was unprepared for his next visit. For some reason he left his bicycle at the bottom of the drive, and we did not hear him approach. I had been discussing spring planting with the Aborigine — now that there were four of us to feed, the garden was an even more important source of food.

The delivery boy appeared suddenly at the door. He held the usual envelope. The Aborigine got up. He knew the boy was in direct contact with the Guests. For a moment the room was very still. I thought then that our stay at the house was over, that we would have to leave immediately. The only other course of action was to silence the boy, and I knew that none of us — with the possible exception of the caretaker — was capable of that.

And then the girl child, who sat as always in the corner of the kitchen, struck one of the caretaker's wooden figures on the floor. Youth First stood at the door, watching. His eyes moved to the object in her hand, a carving that I had taken from the caretaker before it received its hideous final touch. Forgetting his message, the boy crossed the kitchen and squatted in front of the child. She held out the figure. She was offering it as a gift. He took the carving and turned it in his hands. Then he placed it carefully in the orange bag hanging from his shoulder. He retrieved a piece of gleaming obsidian from his pocket.

'Watch,' said the boy. 'You can cut with this.' He took a battered sandwich from the bag, and laid it on his knee. He drew the edge of the volcanic glass across the bread.

'Would you like some?' he said. She nodded, took a square of sandwich and chewed it slowly.

'My sister baked the bread,' he said. 'You can have the rest if you want.' The child nodded again. He gave her the remaining piece of the sandwich and watched her gravely eat his gift. When she had finished, the child put out her hand for the piece of obsidian. The boy pressed it into her palm. The two of them remained like that for a time, the child staring down at the shard of black glass in her hand, the messenger boy kneeling before her, as though mesmerised by the act of exchange. Then he got up and began reluctantly to back away from the child. He was at the door when I called to him.

'The letter.' He looked back in confusion, dropped the message on the table and went out.

I tore open the envelope. The games, stated the note, had been cancelled because of the 'unavailability of selected participants'. We were to 'release captive animals in a controlled manner' and further instructed to replace items prone to deterioration in their containers. New games were to be scheduled at some time in the future.

'They plan to have you back by then,' I said to the Aborigine. He was at the door and looking after the retreating messenger. He turned to the child and extended his hand, palm up.

'Your present. Can I see it?' The child looked at him with her limpid eyes. She shook her head.

'A special favour?' he said. The child did not move. He reached out for the piece of obsidian, and in a swift small movement the child brought the stone across his wrist and laid open the flesh. A filament of blood started out on his black skin. He rubbed it away, and I saw that the cut was quite shallow. Her porcelain face was impassive. The Aborigine stood up and sucked the wound in his wrist. Then he turned to me and grimaced.

'A young priestess,' he said. 'Practising for her first sacrifice.'

The Aborigine and I sat up talking that night. We knew, without further discussion, that there was little danger of the messenger boy betraying us. The bond he had formed with the girl child made us sure of that. I told the Aborigine that I thought he was also safe from the caretaker, who was now dependent on my own presence in order to free himself from the manual labour that he seemed to find so onerous.

The black spoke that night of his home, a house by a dried-up riverbed in the far north of his country, of the rains that came the same week every year, and the bright red soil he worked for crops. He wanted to know, in turn, as much as I could tell him of the city, and the geography of the region. In particular he wished to be told of the slums to the south, of the people who lived there, their customs and the difficulty or otherwise of travelling amongst them. I told him what I knew, much of it information my lover had passed on. Then I talked of Jan and our life beneath the grandstand. I spoke of her ability to describe places she said she had never visited. I brought out the sandalwood box with its fragments of her past, its scents, its branch of black coral.

The Aborigine listened with his head inclined, and occasionally touched his beard. When I had finished, he spread his long fingers on the table. I saw, as though for the first time, the terrible injury that had been inflicted on him.

'The human hand,' he said. 'Bone and sinew. So carefully put together.' He lifted the broken thing off the table. 'With this, I could grind my own lenses, adjust a brass knurled knob, and travel light-years through space.' His hand dropped back. 'Now, to see the bands of Saturn, or the twin suns of Alpha Centauri, I'd need an assistant.' He tried to bunch the fingers into a fist.

'Amputation would have been kinder,' he went on. 'Instead I have half a hand to remind me of the old one.' He looked at me with his black astronomer's eyes. 'And you. It would have been easier if this woman of yours had died in childbirth. Instead you have half a wife.'

I got up and went outside. A canopy of low cloud had settled on the city. The lights of the motorways were reflected in the cloud-base, casting pale fire over the city. A fine rain fell, and the drizzle refracted the glow so that the gates of the stadium might have been the entrance to some inferno. In the industrial suburb nearby the lights of a vehicle appeared. The vehicle seemed to head for the stadium, but when it reached the entrance to the drive it continued down the road and was lost from view behind warehouses. A short while later another vehicle followed the same route.

I imagined Jan out there in the sprawl of suburbs, sheltering, perhaps, in a lean-to or doorway. I thought of the dangers for the homeless in the city — their vulnerability to scouts for the orchards, and to the trade in flesh around the port. The vehicles I had seen now reappeared, retraced their route, and disappeared to the north. I sucked in the cold air to clear my head. Eventually I went inside.

My return to the kitchen coincided with the appearance of the child. She had gone to bed many hours ago, but now she stood at the doorway to the passage.

'I'm thirsty,' she said.

The phrase fell into a deep silence in the room, a silence that seemed to press violently against my ears so that I wondered whether I had imagined her words. The onward movement of time had stopped. The black sat tipped slightly forward, his arm stretched across the table top. He was quite still, a figure in a scene arranged for display. *This is how it is.* The fingers of his good hand curled upward from the table, motioning the girl to approach him. I looked at the child. One arm hung at her side and the other was held across her chest in the manner of an orator. Was she about to make a speech? The onward movement of time had stopped. Her face was in shade. I could not make out which of us she had addressed, or was about to address.

And then I saw the caretaker, who sat on the floor in the corner of the kitchen, his knees drawn up under his chin, his head tipped forward and also obscured by shadow. I thought: The child has come to speak to us, a gathering has been arranged, the audience is assembled. The phrase 'audience is assembled' kept repeating itself in the way that a parasitic phrase cannot be removed from the mind. Except for the recurring words in my head, the onward movement of time had stopped.

But the child did not make a speech, and instead the Aborigine got to his feet.

'Then the thirsty shall drink,' he said. He went to the sink and filled a glass, which he gave to the child. She held it close to her chest and sipped. The glass seemed very large in her small hands. She looked up at the Aborigine.

'How long are you staying?' she said.

'With your permission,' he bowed his head, 'until the future becomes a little more clear.'

She lowered her long eyelashes, finished the water and returned the glass.

'Can't you sleep?' he asked her.

'No.'

The Aborigine said, 'Listen'. He began to speak in his own language, and the music of it ran from his throat like the stream that appeared by his house for one week every year. It was the language of great distance, of cloudless skies and penetrating heat. It took me to the edge of the northern plains, and I heard the birds in the eucalyptus trees by his house, and the creak of the metal roof. I watched the lids of the child become heavy. When the music of his speech came to an end, she spoke, from a distance herself.

'What did you say?'

'I described my home and talked of my daughter. I told you of the books she likes to read, and of her favourite dances.' The child nodded. Then she turned and went like a sleep-walker back down the passage to her room.

9

The sunlight of morning falls through the blinds and onto the wall behind, casting puzzles that are set and continually re-set. A breeze stirs the palms outside, and the shadow of a leaf obscures then recomposes the patterns. A cicada calls, calls again, and is silent.

A child sits at the edge of a garden, while a black in ill-fitting clothes bends to the soil, pulling weeds from among the bright shoots of spring. The child wears an improvised hat, cut from cardboard, to protect her face from the sun. On the veranda, a man with a starched shirt and the hands of a vivisector caresses a device that he has dismantled and put back together now a hundred times. When observed more closely, a scar encircling the mechanic's ankle can be seen to match the pattern of teeth on this machine. Amid the activity the figure of the child is still, a statue set at the side of the garden.

After a time the gardener unbends his frame, stands straight and wipes the sweat from his eyes. He calls then to the mechanic, and in the chamber of the garden, surrounded by palms, the sound is absorbed as soon as it is voiced. The mechanic continues with his task — a spring must attach to a flange, the rotation of jaws must be exact. The gardener calls once more, requesting help to run a line along his seed rows. Again the mechanic does not respond, he is at the climax now of his task. A snap of steel, the circle is complete, and the mechanic walks indoors, disconsolate, a hunter without prey, a man whose time has not yet come.

A black sits at the edge of a garden, his hand a broken bird, while a child in an improvised hat walks amongst spring shoots, carefully, as though estimating the quantity of crops the plot will give up. On the veranda, his face in shadow, squats a master carver, whose fingers move deftly between his legs, and who is surrounded by chips of pale wood.

My father sits at the edge of a garden, while I check the plants for signs of blight. The watcher has a rare concentration, as though trying to recall the location of buried treasure — a bottle of home-made liquor, a coffee pot, the remnants of a dinner suit. At the side of the house, a pile of plywood boxes, stained with the winter rains, are rotting now and collapsing in on themselves. Their presence has never been discussed.

On the veranda a child grips a carving. In the garden I weed another row. On the lawn my keeper wets his lips. In the kitchen the Aborigine bends low to the floor. At the stadium a curve of stand is reflected in a square of black smoked glass.

Towards evening a flight of aircraft in formation crossed the stadium heading towards the mountains. They were very high, and the silver of their fuselages showed as three fine needles in the spring sky. I heard the sound of the aircraft some time before they were visible. The child stood in the garden, her head tipped back, and the Aborigine dropped his hoe and also looked up. The noise of the aircraft was out of all proportion to their size. It descended in waves, each more intense than the one that came before, and filled the stadium with a train of echoes. As the aircraft passed before the sun, a dark shape entered the garden, touched our bodies and was gone.

Later, when dusk descended on the mountains, the trails of the aircraft swung away as blossoms of ice, pointing to the west.

As though satisfied with the proof of her new ability to speak, the child returned to silence. For a while nothing happened in the house or at the stadium, we entered a period when the new arrangements seemed to have been set in glass, and I had the sensation of living through a transparent time, when nothing changed and nothing would ever change, although around us the garden burst into the growth of spring. Each night, the Aborigine told tales to the child at her bedside and afterwards related astronomical stories on the veranda, before leaving for his own bed beneath the slats. Each morning the caretaker carved another crop of his figures, and went about the house with the air of a man who has come upon unexpected wealth. Between dismantling the trap and starching his shirts, he limped each afternoon to the markets, from which he bought food for the household to supplement the crops in our garden.

The child was fully mobile now, and spent much time in the stadium, climbing the stairs and clambering about amongst the upper tiers. It was clear that she wished to explore the stadium alone, and I left her to it, I knew she was capable of looking after herself. She began to spend more time at the stadium than in the house, the stands became a second home to her, and sometimes she would disappear there for a whole day and the Aborigine or I would have to go to retrieve her as dusk fell. I stood in the arena and called, but often she would not respond, and I went searching for her amongst the endless tiers of seats, until I found her standing in some high place with a view of the city, or seated in one of the boxes reserved for spectators of rank. These boxes, smaller than the ministerial box itself, contained upholstered seats, a small refrigerator for refreshments, and viewing glasses on a pivot. One of them had been left unlocked after the last festivities. This was the child's favourite vantage point, it gave an uninterrupted view of the arena.

One afternoon, when the Aborigine had spoken of pain in his mutilated limb, and gone to rest in his den, I sent the caretaker to fetch the child. After an hour, when they had not returned, I went to the stadium myself. I found the pair of them just beyond the main entrance. The caretaker lay face-down in the sand, and the child knelt on his back. She had turned his arm up behind him and gripped his hand in some kind of lock. Her knees were behind his shoulder-blades, and by positioning herself in this way she had been able to pin him to the ground, despite her size. The caretaker's good leg kicked like a cast animal's as he tried to dislodge her, and sand flew up around them in flurries. As I came closer, I saw that the caretaker's face was contorted in a snarl. He could not throw her off — she simply pressed her knees more firmly into his back, and turned his hand a little further in her grip. I stood over the child.

'What are you doing?' I said. The child raised her serious eyes to me, then released the caretaker's hand. She clambered off him and dusted the sand from her clothes. I looked down at the caretaker. Sand had stuck to the saliva around his lips, which gave him the appearance of a child whose face needed cleaning. He was grinning at me, the same expression I had seen a few moments before as a snarl.

'Just a game,' he said. He sat up and wiped the grime from his mouth.

'Yes,' said the child. 'But you're getting too old for games.'

The caretaker began to laugh, the same constricted laugh I had heard once before, a laugh that could be mistaken for sobbing, and within a short time the tears had begun to run on his face and fall into the sand. The child watched without expression, her hands at her sides. When his mirth had played itself out, she turned in a wooden way towards the house, and we followed her back. That night the caretaker shut himself in the bathroom, and did not come out until we had gone to bed.

After this, although I had no reason to believe it was connected with the game in the stadium, the caretaker began to collect old newspapers, either from the market, where the vendors used them to wrap goods, or scavenged from the industrial district, where they had blown down alleys or caught beneath piles of pallets — records of dead years which were distributed free to the population, but seldom even opened by them. The caretaker also ransacked the chests of drawers in the house for their lining paper of ancient newsprint. He became an avid reader of the columns of the Guest press, and for a time, as his new hobby consumed him, even his carving came to a halt. Now it was impossible to walk into the kitchen without coming upon the caretaker bent over the table, turning the sheets of newsprint spread out before him with his manicured hands.

One evening, after the child had gone to bed, and the Aborigine had returned to the stadium, I sat in the kitchen with the caretaker. We had not spoken for several hours, and the only sound was the rustle of the newsprint as my father scanned another page of agricultural reports. The papers on the floor gave off a faint smell of mould. They had been collected that morning from a ruined building in the industrial zone, and according to the caretaker, were the best find he had made all week. In order to mark the occasion he had fashioned an impromptu bow-tie out of a piece of cloth, and sat there before the papers in a newly starched shirt. I had listened to the abrupt announcement of his discovery earlier in the day without comment. For reasons that were unclear to me, my keeper informed me of his collection rituals and his periodic successes.

Now the regular shuffle had stopped. At the table, the care-taker leant forward in his chair, his hands palm-down on the paper before him. He was half-turned away from me, but I could see that his face was white, and yet his neck had become strangely flushed. At first I believed this was because of something in the paper, a piece of news that had alarmed him in some way, although I knew that news of any importance was excluded from the papers. He rocked slightly in his chair and made a thin sound in the back of his throat. And then I looked at the window in front of him and saw the face that was framed there like some strange portrait — its almond eyes, puckered mouth and the chalk-white skin that caught enough of the kitchen light to make it seem to glow beyond the glass.

The face pressed up against the pane. A strip of putty cracked and fell away. As I got to my feet I knew the features were familiar to me, I was struggling to locate them at a point not so far back in my memory and at the moment I reached the kitchen door and threw it open I realised I had been watching a mask that we had packed away that autumn. Apart from the rectangle of light thrown across it by the door, the veranda was in darkness. In front of me stood the child, the mask now pushed up on her head.

'You should be in bed,' I said. She pulled the mask back down over her face. Her voice came to me as though from far away.

'If I go, will you come too?'

'Of course,' I said. She walked through the kitchen, past the caretaker who was standing now by the table, a newspaper crumpled in his hand. I followed the child to her bedroom. She removed the mask, placed it on a chair and climbed into bed. I took off my shoes and she pulled the sheets up over the two of us. I put my arm around her shoulders, and felt her body against mine. She lay there very still, inert and warm, and although her breathing was deep and quiet, I knew that she was not asleep. I thought of the face at the veranda window, and the terror it had evoked in the caretaker. After an hour or so I climbed carefully from the bed.

The Aborigine sat in sunlight next morning and announced his intention to leave for the slums to the south. With the warmth of spring had come new strength, he said, and this time of year was always best for travelling. He had regained much of his weight and his black limbs had a sheen that was new. He took great interest in his body, and spoke to me about it with affection, as though describing a valued friend that I too could come to appreciate if I was prepared to take the time. He showed me the quick of his nails which had turned pink again — evidence of his recovery, he said. He had been cleaning his blackened teeth with a sliver of wood. Now he opened his mouth and instructed me to grip a tooth with my fingers. I took an incisor between finger and thumb. The tooth sat firm in the gum.

He waved away my hand. 'When I arrived,' he said, 'you could have pulled that out of my skull.'

The worst effects of malnutrition, he continued, were on the mind. 'I've known starving men who listened to their thoughts and believed they had invented a strange new language.' He tapped the point of the toothpick on his front teeth. 'They died convinced they were geniuses.'

I saw a flash of orange at the road, and the messenger boy turned into the drive. His hair had been cropped, and as he came towards us I thought that he now resembled a miniature version of our keeper. I found myself searching for the signs of a pierced ear. Youth First dropped his knobbly-tyred bike on the drive, carelessly, and the pedal spun like a top. He came up the steps at a run.

'You're getting an ostrich,' he said, plunging his hand into his bag. We looked on expectantly, half-believing he would produce a bird from its depths. Instead he came out with a large piece of chalk. The Aborigine performed a stretching motion with one leg, and pursed his lips. The messenger boy pretended nonchalance, but his hand was shaking with excitement. 'I saw it at the depot. In a box.' He squatted on the veranda and drew a barred container on the planks. Protruding from the top was a curved neck and a beady-eyed head. We stared at the drawing.

'It is an ostrich, isn't it?' There was a trace of desperation in his voice, and when we still said nothing, I saw again a tear start out in the corner of his eye. The Aborigine cleared his throat.

'Certainly,' he said. 'Or maybe a cassowary. Depending on the number of toes. Definitely not a dromedary.' The boy blinked away the tear, and glared up at the Aborigine.

'Of course it's not a bloody dromedary,' he said.

'Anything's possible,' said the Aborigine, and coughed self-deprecatingly. 'Although it's true that dromedaries are a bit thin on the ground in these parts. But then so are ostriches.'

'What does "thin on the ground" mean?'

The Aborigine smiled. 'Your friend is at the stadium. Why don't you go and interrogate *her*?' The boy looked down at his drawing, then rubbed out a section of the bird and lengthened the neck.

'It's big,' he said seriously. 'And cries out.' Then he handed me the message envelope, and went down the steps. He rode off towards the stadium. We watched until he had disappeared through the main entrance.

I said, 'You know how children work.'

'I know how children used to work.' He inserted the toothpick between his teeth.

'Where are your own children now?'

'With their tribe,' he said, frowning, and then fell silent. After a time he got up and walked back into the house.

The envelope contained a document headed 'Live Delivery — Advance Advice' and gave details of arrival date and feeding regime. It did not specify the type of animal, or what part it would take in the games.

That night in a dream the carcass of a great bird, its rib-cage flayed and the skin stripped from its skull, cavorted in the arena, while around it a wind of fine sand blew in the open pan of the stadium. The animal was dead, I told myself, it shouldn't be able to run around like this, but the drama persevered, taunting me to imagine its outcome, until I woke with a piece of iron at my heart and the flint-like sound of a beak at the window. I got up and secured the blind cord that slapped the glass, but I could no longer sleep, and lay through four hours of darkness until the dawn light grew weakly at the edges of the blinds.

Some days later a flat-backed delivery truck drove up to the house. On the tray sat an aluminium cage, barred at the front and covered in netting. A bird I had never seen stood inside, fixing us with a wild eye and dipping its head from time to time. Beside the cage lay sacks of grain. I asked the driver where it had come from. 'How would I know?' he replied. After lifting the cage from the tray he drove away without speaking further.

'Not an ostrich. An emu,' said the Aborigine instantly when he saw the bird. He stood beside the cage after the truck had disappeared and spoke to the bird as he spoke to the child, seriously and in his own tongue. The creature turned its sharp head a little on one side, as though listening intently to what he had to say.

'I offered my sympathy,' he said later. 'And told her I knew exactly how she felt.'

In the evening I found the Aborigine and the caretaker seated opposite each other at the kitchen table. The black was leafing through the pile of discarded papers.

'Dull,' he said. 'Very dull.' The caretaker went on with his task. He did not pause or look up. The Aborigine waved a paper at me as I came in. 'And despite this month's celestial extravagance, not even a map of the night sky.'

The papers looked quite recent, which was a new departure for the caretaker. Until now he had concentrated on newspapers at least several years old, and often much older than that. The extravagance the black spoke of had been explained to me patiently during the week. A comet was visiting the southern skies, an event which occurred perhaps twice each century.

The Aborigine had produced his toothpick, and was probing his gums. Suddenly he spoke to the caretaker.

'What happened to your ear?' The caretaker glanced up, moistened his lips and went back to his newspaper. I saw that his fingers were smudged with ink from the endless turning of pages.

The Aborigine looked at me and made a comical gesture with his eyebrows. He cleared his throat. 'And why do you cut your hair like a convict?' he went on. The caretaker folded the newspaper he was reading.

'Is this an interrogation?' he said.

'If you like. Pretend . . .' The Aborigine made a dry gesture with his mutilated hand, '. . . pretend I'm the Hotel Manager.' The caretaker was suddenly very still. He stared at the Aborigine as though seeing him for the first time.

'What do you know about the Hotel Manager?'

'Like you, I am an ex-patron.'

The caretaker's voice shook. 'An ex-patron?'

'Perhaps no one is ever really an *ex*-patron. The hospitality of the place stays with us.'

'What are you talking about?' I said. 'I cut his ear.' The Aborigine inserted the sliver of wood into the gap left by a missing tooth.

'Is that so?' He looked at me with new interest. 'And yet, nevertheless, I was able to tell a patron, an ex-patron, when I saw one.' He turned back to my father. 'And how long were you accommodated?' The caretaker got abruptly to his feet and walked from the room. The Aborigine watched him go with his black eyes.

'A man who has difficulty with the past,' he said.

'That is a common problem,' I said. The Aborigine walked to the centre of the room, then stretched out on his back on the floor. He raised a leg until it stood perfectly upright from his body, and lowered it again. He repeated the action with the other leg. Then he placed his hands beneath his hips, hoisted his pelvis off the floor, and began to execute a slow bicycle action with his legs.

'Here we are, at the bottom of the world, bicycling backwards into the future,' he said.

'Is that some kind of riddle?' I said.

'Where the eclipse of life is a constant possibility, it is important to keep a sense of the farcical nature of things.' In a single smooth movement he lowered his pelvis to the floor, rolled forward and leaped to his feet.

'Olé!' he shouted, and held his hands above him like a dancer. He performed a slow pirouette, and then bent to the floor in a gracious sweep.

'Now,' he said, 'please do the same.'

I lay down on my back.

'Your hands . . . there . . . correct. Now, point at the light-bulb with your toe . . . lower your foot, and repeat with the other toe.' He watched me for some time, and then said, 'Are you impressed with the farcical nature of things?'

'Yes,' I said.

'Good,' he said. 'In that case the lesson is complete.'

10

Now the caretaker began a human figure, cut, unusually, from dark wood and larger than his previous work. As always he left the features of the face until last, but despite the absence of this detail the subject was clear very early. The limbs of the figure were long and fine, and one of the hands was transformed at the wrist into a formless club. My father took great care over the genitals, which were out of all proportion to the size of the figure. The phallus stood erect and jutting, so that the carver was forced to attach a base to the carving to prevent it toppling forward.

'Is this an act of homage?' murmured the Aborigine, as he observed the figure on the window-sill. 'Should I be flattered?'

'I don't think so,' I said.

'A work of lust, then?'

'Possibly.' I described my father's bathroom rituals, which it seemed the Aborigine had not yet witnessed. He went to the carving and turned it in his hand.

'Studying the religions of the east,' he said, 'I read about these figures. Fertility gods. I'm happy to be counted amongst them. Like all those called to the cloth, my real desire was for immortality.'

Outside came the sound of splintering wood, and I walked through the house to a side window. Directly beneath me, the caretaker was demolishing the plywood boxes that lay beside the house with an axe. The child stood some distance off, on the waste-ground between the house and the stadium, watching intently. On the colder days of winter we had built fires in the kitchen range, but those days were well past, and the caretaker had no reason to cut firewood now. The child ran towards the axe-man, then halted a few metres away. The rise and fall of the implement slowed and stopped.

The child spoke to him, but what she said was inaudible. Then she walked off and stood observing once more from a distance. Now she wore the mask that had surprised me at the window. Even from this distance the features were quite vivid, a face of startled innocence, too big for the wearer, so that from where I stood she appeared as a stick creature with an outsized head. The axe resumed its arc, and for a while the stick-figure watched, and I listened, as the pile of boxes that had sat there for so long was reduced to matchwood. When he had finished his destruction of the caskets, my father stood panting beneath the window, unaccustomed as he was to physical activity.

Out on the waste-land the messenger boy drew up on his bicycle beside the child and removed an object that had been fixed to his handlebars. It was a tiny windmill. He dismounted his bicycle, and began to run a circle around the masked figure, holding the windmill aloft on a cane. The child turned on the spot, following the running figure, observing the toy, until the entertainer finished his show. Then solemnly, as they had done once before, they exchanged gifts: the child removed the mask and held it out to the boy, then he took the present, placed it in his bag, and offered the windmill in return. Shortly afterwards the pair of them disappeared from view, walking in the direction of the stadium.

Later that afternoon I discovered the child and her companion in the ring. They had manoeuvred the messenger's bicycle between the ropes, and he rode in tight circles around the centre, the mask pulled down over his head, watched by the child from one corner. As I came closer I could hear the flat whirr of the windmill fixed to his handlebars. I climbed up beside the child, and as I did so the messenger boy began a shrill, high sound that rose and fell like a siren.

The boy, perhaps distracted by my arrival, and unsighted by the mask, wobbled a little, then collided with the ropes bounding the ring. The bicycle slewed over, and the boy tumbled sideways across the floor. I helped him to his feet. The mask had twisted down around his neck, and his eyes were very bright. 'Are you hurt?' He shook his head, readjusted the mask and climbed back onto his bike. The windmill had been knocked askew. He straightened the toy and adjusted its fastening. Then he set off again on his circle, his head low over the handlebars, his voice rising again to a shrill scream.

I remembered then the first time I had met him. I recalled how he had blown the lock of hair from his eyes as he approached me on the veranda, the angry way he spoke of the sunset and of the foreigners who were being prepared for the games. He was different now, he had lost his orphan's eyes, and his hands no longer trembled when he spoke.

In the kitchen, the caretaker and the black faced each other across the table. They were motionless, but between them stood the carving of the Aborigine. They gripped the figure with great concentration, as though each was trying to wrest it from the other. I remained at the door, watching. The caretaker held the carving at the base of the torso, so that his hand enclosed the thighs, while the Aborigine gripped the figure higher up, around its bony chest. I could hear stretching sinew, and I thought: If this continues, neither of them will win, and the carving will be destroyed.

A breeze came through the kitchen window and the pages of a newspaper beside the caretaker turned in a flurry. Arranged along the window-sill, like a queue of prisoners, a line of figurines looked down on the scene. At the stadium, the messenger whirled on his bike. In the ring the child followed his path. In its cage the emu strutted and called. At the door I watched and listened.

Slowly, unhooking one finger at a time, the Aborigine loosed his grip on the carving. He turned his palms up on the table to indicate defeat. The caretaker drew the figure across the table to him, like a chess player returning his queen to home rank. The Aborigine raised his head.

'A victory for the idolaters,' he said. There was a silence, and he got to his feet.

'I thought you were happy to be carved,' I said. He massaged his knuckles.

'I've changed my mind.' I watched him cross to the window. Out on the waste-land, the emu's head protruded from the cage. She seemed to squint in our direction and her harsh cry came once again.

'The creature is hungry,' said the black. He looked down at the carving, as though reluctant to abandon it to his adversary, then he turned and left the kitchen. I watched him walk, head bowed, across the waste-land to the cage, his hand held against him like an injured wing.

The caretaker remained crouched over the carving. He was rocking slightly in his chair, as though attempting to annul some pain. A line of perspiration had travelled from his temple to his collar. He ran his tongue over his lips.

'How much longer is he staying?'

'You heard him — "Until the future is more clear".'

'That could be some time,' he said. I sat down opposite the caretaker. He held the carving to his chest and stroked the wood with the palm of his hand.

'Do you see how he retires into his beauty?' he said.

'Who?'

'The nigger.' He traced the line of the figurine's limbs. 'We sit here, stewing in our semen, *while he retires into his beauty*.' I watched the rhythmic caressing of the figure.

'How long were you held in the Hotel?'

'What is it to you?'

'I'm interested in the place.'

My father got up from the table and walked to the window. It was clear he had stopped listening to me. He placed the Aborigine at the head of the queue of his carvings, then squatted on his heels so that he could run his eye down the line of figures. He addressed his wooden offspring, gesturing to them as to an audience.

'I once held a position of influence. To see me now you might not believe this. However, it's true.' He squinted at the carvings.

I thought: He's expecting them to respond. There was a long silence.

'May I reply on their behalf?' I said. He ignored me, and continued to peer at the figures.

' "We are flattered to be informed of this fact",' I said. ' "And regret to see that you have fallen on such hard times. However there are some questions we would like to ask about our own future".'

He turned from the carvings and stood up. 'You think you can speak for them?' he said harshly. He walked to the open door and indicated the stadium.

'You'll perform in that place one day,' he said. 'They'll put you on show.' He fingered his suit trousers. 'But they'll dress you up first.'

'Like you.'

He nodded. 'Possibly. But it's more likely that you will have your own costume.'

I placed my hand on the stack of yellowed newsprint. 'What is in these papers?'

'The past.'

I shook my head. 'There are only lies. And agricultural reports.'

'The past is there for those who look.'

'Which past?'

113

'There is only one past.' His voice had become strained.

' "There Is Only One Past",' I mimicked. ' "The Guest looks after his Host".'

I saw the bright blade of his penknife. He held it in his outstretched hand as though offering it as a gift, and yet I knew that he was not offering it as a gift. I moved away. There was a tension in his body that I had not seen before. For a moment I was certain that he was going to attack me. He put his hand to his mutilated ear, and the weapon dropped to his side and lay at the sharp crease of his trousers. He stood like that for a time, swaying slightly on his feet, then turned and limped from the room.

Later, on impulse, I found the flute that had lain untouched for so long. The instrument had been damaged in its fall, but I worked the keys and found it still playable. I went to the arena and climbed up into the main stand. Evening light flooded the place and illuminated the structure of the stadium with great sharpness; the cantilevered roofs, layers of seating, and the metal doors giving onto the arena. A lagoon of mauve ebbed across the sand.

In the boxing ring, still lit by sunlight, the child stood beside the messenger boy. Their game appeared to be over. I played a few notes on the flute and the sound floated into the arena, then returned as a delicate echo. I thought: The child has not heard the instrument since the day of her birth. In the ring, the child and her companion looked up. They stood slightly apart, minute figures in the gulf of the stadium. Then the boy lowered his bicycle through the ropes of the ring, climbed onto the seat and rode away across the sand. He had to stand on his pedals to make progress on the resisting surface. As he reached the main entrance, he looked back once before disappearing from view.

I began another tune, whose name I knew to be 'Lilliburlero'. I had a clear recollection of my mother performing this tune in a sunlit room of my childhood, and as I played the opening notes I could see her, a slim figure with shining chestnut hair, and see the line of her throat as she lifted her head to sing. The melody came easily, and when I leapt an octave to the chorus, the clear notes rose in the stadium, and I knew from the stillness of the child in the ring that the sound of the instrument was familiar to her, and that at that moment she was returning to the instant of her birth on a humid morning when the pure tones of the flute had last rung out — when the surgeon's knife and the spreading stain of fresh bright blood had signalled the start of her own strange journey in the world and the end of her mother's fragile grasp on the present.

The shadow of the stand was encroaching upon the ring, and now the child was invisible, absorbed into the gloom. After a while I descended the long stairway. She had left the ring, and I followed her back to the house.

The Aborigine became silent now, something had changed since his confrontation with the caretaker. He still performed his exercises, and continued his observation of the stars, but he avoided conversation and would not reply to questions. In the evening he sat at the kitchen table and wrote in a notebook, his long sloping hand marching through the pages, but what he wrote was gibberish to me, I took it to be the language of his tribe. Once I joked with him about letters home, but he looked at me blankly, as at a stranger, and returned to his book. During the day he spent much time with the emu, leaning with his forearms on the bars of her cage, and then one afternoon he made up a leg rope for the animal and set her loose. After that she would strut and call at the end of the rope, while the Aborigine sat deep in thought, clasping his knees, just beyond the range of her powerful claws. Once, I heard him address the bird in his own language, but in general he was as silent with the creature as he was with the rest of us.

Although the Aborigine no longer spoke to us, he did not

shun us as he did my father. If the caretaker entered the room, it was only a matter of time before the Aborigine gathered up his things and left. This became a ritual, in which the caretaker also played his part. My father would return from the markets, unload the meagre supplies from a plastic bag and stock the kitchen cupboards. While the caretaker completed his chores, the black went on with his writing, but as soon as my father was finished, and made to settle in the kitchen, he would close his book and move outside to the veranda. There he would recline in a broken chair, his feet on the rail, and roll a cigarette of dried herbs from the garden. I often sat beside him, watching the glowing tip, observing his silent investigation of the heavens. If the caretaker strayed onto the veranda himself, the black would grind the cigarette under his heel and go off down the steps into the night.

Perhaps in revenge at this treatment, the caretaker took great care over the final stages of the carving. He accentuated the broken teeth and fashioned a low-slung chin and deep-set eyes to match the caricatured mouth. He had never spent so much time on a figure, and although the features were deformed, the carving was so finely worked that I thought I had never seen anything so beautiful. On completion he placed it in the bathroom, where it stood like a god in some white tiled shrine. When I lay in the bath and looked up at the alcove where it rested, all that was visible through the rising vapour was the phallus of black jutting wood.

One morning the Aborigine failed to come in for breakfast and I went to his den and found his exercise book and candles gone. I knew then he had left us during the night. I walked to the bottom of the drive and looked up and down the road. The morning was hot, the first day of summer, and away to the west a cloud bank boiled above the ranges. I crossed the road and went on into the industrial zone, half-believing I might come upon the black, that he might have risked a daylight walk. I had rarely been in this part of the city during daylight, and I was struck by the colour of the warehouses, a uniform cream, as though they were all part of the same rambling complex. At a silent, baking intersection I came upon a bicycle which had been crushed by the passage of a fast-moving vehicle. Beyond the bicycle, a pair of wire spectacles, one lens still intact, looked up from the gutter with silent fury. Further down the road lay an object that seemed familiar. I went closer and saw that it was a human forearm. A pin of metal pierced the elbow and was secured to a leather strap. I bent down and saw the arm was made of drab pink plastic. I steered the thing into the gutter with my toe, and turned back towards the house.

Later that evening, when it was clear the Aborigine was gone for good, I went into the bedroom where the child sat up in her night-gown. Above us the woman in the swamp looked down with her timeless, empty smile. The painting should be removed, I thought, it had been there long enough. The child leaned forward in her bed.

'Will he be back?' she said.

'I don't think so,' I said. 'At least, not out of choice.' She looked at me for a time with her clear green eyes, then lowered them to her lap and sighed like an old woman. I watched her clasp and unclasp her small hands, and then she rested her chin on her chest and slipped into a reverie that might have been a trance. When after a time I touched her shoulder to rouse her, she blinked at me with glassy eyes, and I left her, a small figure in her bed, tracking her lost adviser in some unknowable landscape of the childhood mind.

When the caretaker was told the news, he strode about the house, opening doors, picking up objects and discarding them, and hovering over his newspapers as though they might hold the key to the Aborigine's sudden departure. Then he swept all his figurines into a box and went off across the waste-land to the store-sheds. Next he went through each room in the house with a broom, trying, it seemed, to remove all trace of the black from his mind. For days he walked about in agitation, his hobbies abandoned and his face working and strained. He spent long periods in his bathroom shrine, and on the few occasions that I was able to get into the place, I found dried flowers beside the figure of the Aborigine, and once, a small pile of nail parings that I knew to be from the caretaker's own manicured hands.

The carving became the centre of my father's daily routines. In the morning he washed before his familiar, and in the evenings it watched over his solitary sexual acts. I heard him there, late into the night, the whisper of some incomprehensible monologue and the rhythmic creak of boards. In the mornings I found him on the bathroom floor, sleeping off the exertions of the night. The caretaker had always been a wiry man, fit and well-muscled for his age, but I began to suspect his privations would make him ill. He had become pale, and no longer shaved his head. His trousers lost their crease, and the shirts he had so carefully bleached became grey and stained with sweat. One day I stopped him as he entered his shrine. If he continued like this, I told him, he would damage his health.

'What would you know of illness?' he whispered, and bolted the bathroom door against me.

In the weeks that followed the departure of the Aborigine, the child spent more time in the banana grove, crouching in the lean aquarium light, or staring up at the fruit that never ripened. Her complexion still had the perfection of a doll, but her limbs were stronger and she no longer moved with the awkwardness of a child.

'Where are the bananas?' she asked me once when I found her kneeling at the base of a palm.

'Fruit don't grow much in the wild, any more,' I said.

'Why not?'

I shrugged. 'You find them in the plantations. That is where they live.' From the direction of the stadium came the drumming cry of the emu. The child turned her head.

'Everything is caged,' she said.

'Not everything. There are the river dogs, and . . . some birds.' The child looked at me in silence. 'In the south,' I went on, 'there are plains and mountains. Open space for wild animals.'

'How do you know?'

'Everyone knows about the south,' I said, lamely.

'Have you been there?'

I shook my head, and as I looked into those eyes, I was certain then that the mythical south would remain just that, and none of us would get to see the country I spoke of — the plains, running streams, and groves of apricot trees. It was clear to me then that our futures were tied to the stadium, and however much we might wish to leave — the Aborigine who even now fled south, the child, the caretaker, my absent lover — all of us had been touched by the place, there was no escaping it, we had been drawn to the arena to take part in some matter whose form was obscure, but which was tied to the meanings of the impenetrable times in which we lived.

— III —

11

The first of my lovers in that early period, the travelling years, was a girl my own age, unable to speak, but with a mobile face that made such handicap irrelevant — at least for the purposes we required of each other. We had stopped at an abattoir, a building that stood on a plain near a river and which had fallen into disrepair. I remember us entering the place, the desolation of it, and of my companion touching my shoulder and pointing to the crows that nested under the roof. Whether the girl had been born dumb, or had dumbness thrust upon her, I did not know, it was all the same to me, and with time her silence seemed more natural than speech. She had a tongue, that I knew, and in the chill mornings in our fallen abattoir, she put it to uses I did not know existed. I could not recall the whole of her, only certain glancing gifts; her clear violet eyes, a tiny mole, the pattern of sunlight on her wrist.

Now, in the weeks after the Aborigine's departure, that abattoir returned to me often, the interior of the shed, its chutes and gates and hanging chains, and our home in one corner, a makeshift pen we built to keep away the cold. Much of that time was confused in my mind, the hunger and silence and rhythms of exhausted sex, and for a while in that killing place I thought I would die myself, the reek of death and sex had come upon me like a gas, it was a dank season and we had gone on like that for months, chilled and fucking to stay alive, it seemed at times.

As the summer of the games rose again in that place beside the stadium, I had the same sense of blood in the air, the grating of soil, and despite the days of heat, I felt the cold of that abattoir from years before, it would not leave me, the atmosphere of that half-forgotten place intruded on the present. There was no air to breathe in the city that summer, the hot days stretched out as the year crawled to its end. Spring winds had stopped with the onset of the heat, and a fine dust settled over the house and the stadium. It was hard to know where this dust originated, for weeks there had been not so much as a breath of wind. To the west the mountains appeared far off, as though viewed through glass on which a film had formed. The kitchen table had to be wiped before each meal, and I would see the child bent over a surface where the grime had fallen, her lips moving soundlessly, tracing shapes with her finger in the dust.

There was an aging of things, which owed something to the accumulation of dust. The lost past of the place pressed down upon its contents, and when I looked at the objects around me, they appeared to have been there for longer than was possible. The painting in the child's room (which I had still not removed) was one such example. The skin of the woman, the colour of the cloth at her waist, had a familiarity that I could not explain, and which went beyond the fact that I had looked at this painting perhaps a hundred times since I arrived in the place.

With the approach of the games, I went to the store-sheds to examine the equipment. We had packed it away carefully, and apart from a covering of dust that had filtered into the boxes, the material had come through the winter in good shape. I had forgotten how much had been stored there — many tonnes in all, I guessed. There were costumes and great rolls of printed cloth. There was electrical equipment: floodlights, thick coils of cabling, and consoles wrapped carefully in plastic. I recalled the caretaker's description of the technicians who arrived at a stadium shortly before games were to begin. He had said they went from stadium to stadium in a gang. Years earlier, on our way to the city from the country, Jan and I had been waiting near a motorway when a convoy of vehicles passed by. One of the vehicles, marked 'Entertainment Servicing', had pulled into a siding. The passengers, all women and dressed in similar clothing, got out to exercise. They were young, about our own age, and had stretched their limbs with the discipline of a well-drilled team. We had watched them for some time, drawn by the economy of their movements.

Now, in one of his rare moments away from the the bathroom, I asked the caretaker when he expected the first visit.

'The place is clean,' he said thickly. 'They won't come until a few days before the opening ceremony. They'll have done the choreography, and apart from the technical work, there will be little left to arrange.'

'Choreography?'

'They demand the highest standards of co-ordination.' He looked at me with a stony face. 'They're great art-lovers.'

'They're fond of animals, too,' I said.

'Animals?'

'And children,' I said. 'To tell the truth, the scope of their affection is boundless.'

He frowned. 'They're not keen on blacks.'

'Give them time,' I said. 'They'll look back and see them differently. They'll feel sentimental about them.' The caretaker steepled his hands on the dusty table.

'I don't like your tone,' he said. I leaned over and gripped his remaining earlobe.

'I don't like yours. In fact, there are a lot of things I don't like about you. I've sometimes been tempted to finish you off.'

He flexed his leg beneath the table. 'Your own father?'

'Who said you were my father?'

He laughed 'You did. In your sleep. You spend half the night telling us. You're my son. I'm your father.' He stood up and began to shuffle around the floor of the kitchen, and it was some time before I realised that he was performing a dance of sorts. He began to chant, a parody of the Aborigine's nasal evening song.

'*Father's son, father's son, and we're all together when the roof falls in.*'

When he finished, I said, ' "Father's sin" would rhyme better.'

He laughed again, a trace of hysteria in his voice now, and renewed his chant, his arms working at his side.

'*The sins of the father shall be visited upon the sons. Honour thy father and thy mother that thy days shall be long in the land that the lord giveth thee.*'

I watched him for a time without speaking. Then I said, 'Do you know about my mother?'

'Why should I?'

'You said you once held a position of rank. Perhaps you know what became of her.'

The caretaker walked to the window and looked out into the night. He turned then and limped to the bathroom.

'How would I know if I'd even met her?' he snarled, and went on into his shrine.

We relied on our keeper for food from the markets, and in his present state he had little energy for the trip. He had reduced his visits to twice a week, and then set out only after coaxing and returned with a poor selection of goods. Once, when I had been afraid he would miss the main Saturday market, I went into the bathroom and dragged him from his shrine. At times, I considered removing the statue and burying it in the garden, but I was uncertain of the effect this would have on the man.

I sat on the veranda in the evenings, planning the food requirements for the week, and thought of the coming Christmas feasts. Pickings would be good in a few weeks when the carcasses were put out in sacks along the streets of the northern suburbs. I remembered that first Christmas beneath the grandstand, the meals of mutton-bird beneath the slats, the rustle of tin foil and the grease on our fingers. And I thought of my lover, the salt of her neck and the texture of her skin . . . those odd eyes that could look so distant and yet so close.

The box containing her things lay in the living-room, unopened now except for the occasions when the child asked to see inside. She would go through its contents carefully, placing each object on the floor, and stop at the piece of coral, turning it in her hand. I told her the coral was made up of long dead creatures, and described the reef in the ocean to the west from where it had come. She brushed her fingertips across it, gently, with the sober look of someone who has never seen the sea.

At the warehouses, activity had begun with the early harvest, and from the veranda I could hear the noise of the trucks. In the evenings I would catch the scent of some new fruit, carried to me on the night air, and hear the sound of great doors closing on a crop that would soon be sent abroad. One morning about this time the messenger boy went with the child to explore the stadium. At lunchtime I was looking through the equipment at the store-rooms, and found a case containing masks had been opened, and a number of them missing. I went in search of the children. The arena was empty and the stadium silent. I scanned the tiers for signs of movement, and then climbed the stairs to the girl child's favourite vantage point. The door of the box was open. The place was deserted, but the child's piece of black obsidian lay on the floor, and beside it, a pile of masks, neatly stacked. I bent to pick them up, and heard the door behind me close quietly. I crossed to the viewing window in the door and looked out. When I tried the handle it would not move.

After a while a mask appeared at the window, the black minstrel face with exaggerated lips and white-ringed eyes. The window was too high off the floor for the wearer to be either of the children. It could only be the caretaker.

'You should be at the market,' I said. The face pressed forward against the glass, causing its features to distort, then withdrew and watched me with startled eyes. I felt suddenly light-headed, as though I had been returned to a dream.

'Is this a game?'

'No,' said the mask.

'What is it?'

'A performance.' I strained to recognise the voice, which was muffled by the mask.

'How can it be? You haven't done anything except stand there.' My own voice sounded thin and unconvincing.

'That's because we need a narrator.' I put a hand against the wall of the box. I was aware of the texture of its surface beneath my palm. There was a tightness in my head. I found myself speaking to a void in which a solitary star shone as a distant point of light.

'Where will you get one?

'We want you,' said the mask. My words came back to me across the void, as though spoken by someone else.

'But I don't know the story.'

Outside, the face dropped from view. A few seconds later the door opened. The girl child stood there solemnly with someone I had never seen before, a girl a little taller with a mass of curly red hair. Freckles flecked her cheeks and the bridge of her nose. The children stood hand in hand. A moment before, I realised, one had been standing on the other's shoulders. Now, I could not tell who had been behind the mask, which lay at their feet.

'Did we fool you?' said the red-haired child. I nodded. Her voice was deep and clear, like a chime.

'We thought so.' She made an apologetic gesture. 'You don't look as though you're easily fooled.'

'Thank you.'

'You didn't seem to enjoy it very much.'

'I thought you were someone else.'

'The carver?' she said. I nodded. 'I know him from the market,' she went on. 'He's always there, looking for food.' I could see that the red-haired girl was much older than her companion, although there was little between them in height. They had the manner of people who had known each other for some time. I turned to the girl child.

'Where did you meet your friend?' She bent her head in the direction of the ring. 'She came with Youth First?' She nodded again, an almost imperceptible movement. 'And where is he?' I asked. She shrugged and folded her hands, the faintest of smiles on her lips. I went to the pile of masks and picked them off the floor. I adopted a serious manner.

'These are in our custody. We have to ensure that all props are taken care of. Any damage will be noticed and assessed. What the organisers would do in such circumstances is hard to say. They'd probably take the matter very seriously.'

The red-haired child turned from the window. She held up the mask. 'Why don't you try it on?' she said in a reasonable voice.

From the arena came the howl of a river dog. The child continued to look up at me without blinking, holding the mask before her. I walked to the front of the box. Far below, in the ring, the messenger boy circled on his bicycle, a pennant flying from the frame. Following him was a river dog, a rangy specimen with black fur and a long stride. The boy had got up enough speed to outpace the dog, who remained the same distance behind him. Round and round they went. It did not seem to occur to the dog to cut across the ring and head off his quarry. Even from this distance I could hear the faint sound of a hooter on the bicycle.

I turned back to the children, who waited there unmoving, the red-haired child still holding up the mask. The girl child stood with her hands clasped behind her, eyes cast down, as though averting them out of some kind of propriety. I had a sudden desire to laugh.

I sat down on the upholstered seat and crossed my arms. I sensed that in some way I was on trial.

'I don't think that mask would suit me,' I said. 'It looks better on you.'

'Don't be silly,' said the red-haired child. Her tone was measured, friendly.

'And when I put on the mask, what then?'

The girl shrugged. 'You have to start somewhere,' she said. The desire to laugh returned. I got up abruptly.

'Don't you think its time we rescued your friend?' I said.

The messenger boy had no wish to be rescued, and by the time I arrived at the ring, the dog was ready to drop. It stood in one corner, watching the boy on his bicycle. Saliva ran from the animal's tongue and writhed briefly on the metal before evaporating. The dog's legs were splayed, as though barely able to support the body.

Nearby, the cyclist circled, one eye on the dog. He glanced up when I came to the ring.

'I thought you might need help,' I said. He looked at me scornfully, and sounded his hooter. The dog winced. It swayed slightly on its legs.

'What are you doing to this animal?' Youth First continued to circle on his bike, holding the handlebars with one hand. He ran his free hand through his hair.

'Training it,' he said. I raised my eyebrows, but he was engaged in some manoeuvre on his machine. He leaned back on the bicycle and let go of the handlebars. The front wheel of the bicycle lifted off the floor of the ring. He completed a circuit in this way. 'I'm also training myself,' he said in a loud voice. When he had completed his performance, he slipped a hand into his message bag.

'Do you want some fruit?' Without waiting for an answer, he threw me a clump of dark orange material, which consisted of small objects stuck together. I chewed on the fruit, the flavour sharp on my tongue. Tyres hissed on the metal surface. I began to feel a slight euphoria, a haze at the back of my skull. I looked up into the stadium. The oval of the stands arched above me, an encircling hand. A flock of birds, black against the sky, appeared over the roofs. They dispersed and reformed like a knot being tied and retied. At my feet the dust had become thicker. The wheels of the bicycle and the paws of the dog made little impression, the marks seemed to be filling already.

I got down on my knees in front of the dog. Its tongue was large and out of proportion and its eyes were glazed with tiredness. I was aware of different-coloured hair on its muzzle. Black and pepper brown. Its head drooped. A few drops of saliva fell soundlessly to the ring. As I got nearer to him, the dog backed against the ropes. It lifted a paw as if in greeting, but I knew this was a defensive gesture brought on by exhaustion.

Above me the birds had settled closer to the arena. The flock became distinct individuals now, and formed a mass only briefly before flying apart again. Shapes moved at the edge of my vision. I had a sense of shadows among the tiers, as though the stadium was being filled with life. I heard the beating of wings. I got close to the dog and looked into his yellow eyes. I could feel his breath on my face. The creature made a human noise, a kind of chewing, in the back of its throat. I put out a hand and touched it, and the dog lifted its head. In the depths of those yellow eyes, running backwards through the generations of his ancestors, I could see the thread of its breeding, the intricate train of hatred implanted by our masters. I thought of its tribe, many of whom would have appeared in this venue over the years, and a number of whom, I was sure, had performed in this ring. Overhead, the beating had become intense, and I felt the movement of air on my back. The dog sank to its knees, and birds formed a dark cover above us, stirring the dust. I could hear a rising clamour, the roar of an impatient crowd. Then, as suddenly as they had descended, the birds rose away from us and the sound of their wings receded.

I got to my feet. The boy had dismounted and stood beside me. He also gazed at the dog.

'He's come a long way,' he said.

'In his training?'

The boy turned to me, amused. 'You can't train river dogs,' he said. 'From the river. He's come a long way from the river, and he won't be able to find his way back.'

Above us, the birds had risen well above the ring, and were almost lost in the burning sky. Youth First found a length of twine in his bag. He looped it around the neck of the exhausted animal and led it from the ring. He tied the free end of the twine to his bicycle. 'Back to the river,' he murmured. He climbed on the machine and rode off across the sand with the dog following behind him.

In the stands, the children were descending the concrete stairway. The red-haired child held the pile of masks in her arms. When they reached the arena floor they stopped and looked towards the ring. Then they turned in the direction of the entrance, and followed the boy and his dog to the turnstiles; the girl child in front, her companion behind her with the masks, a procession of small figures crossing the sand. Faintly, as though from a distance, I heard strains of music, a band playing somewhere far off, a tune that was half-familiar but unnameable. When I turned my head to catch it more clearly, there was only silence, and although I listened intently, it did not come again.

12

That night, as I lay asleep beneath the gaze of the woman in red, I travelled to the edge of the dreaming city and met my lover in an open field. She sat on a rock, watching me with a look of distant regret. It was some time before I realised the significance of this look, and noticed her eyes were the same colour — dull green, the colour of the dead. She wore a coat that was too small, so that the sleeves rode up at the wrists. 'Why don't you get a new coat?' I asked her, and she smiled her mocking smile.

'This is my dancing coat,' she said. She stood up on the rock, and I saw that she was about to perform. She made a pirouette, and then another in quick succession. When she had completed her dance she curtsied and sat down.

'You're a mother. You shouldn't be out here dancing,' I said. She looked at me with amusement.

'Mothers just fade away,' she said. 'Don't you know that?' I sat near the rock for some time, trying to relate her reply to what I had just said.

'They still have their uses,' I assured her. I was aware of a deep pain in my chest, below the breastbone, which had come from nowhere, and which I recognised, suddenly, as loss.

The person I was speaking to was no longer Jan, but was my own mother. The coat seemed even smaller on her than it had on my lover.

'Why don't you get a new coat?' I repeated.

'This is my dying coat,' said my mother. 'You should think of getting one for yourself.'

'No,' I said. 'I plan to go on for a while yet.' My mother got off the rock and walked away across the field. She seemed offended by my reply.

When I woke, I found that the sheet had coiled around me, and for some time before I freed myself I was trapped and immobile on the bed, like a body caught up in a shroud.

The still days of summer continued, and the dust that settled on the stadium had dampened all sound, so that it seemed at times the place was subsiding into a final silence. I took to wearing a handkerchief around my face outdoors, but the dust settled in my hair and inside my clothing, and I had to bath each day to wash off the grime. The western mountains had been obscured for months now, and I considered the idea that the dust signalled some permanent change in the climate of the city.

The children came and went at the ring, while the games moved inexorably closer. I spent my days beneath the stadium, unpacking equipment and laying it out on the tables in preparation. I had given up trying to keep the materials away from the children, who removed various items for their play. Outside the emu strutted in its compound and cocked its head in anger if anyone approached. At night its cry was audible in the house, but even this too seemed muted in our dust-bound world.

In the bathroom the caretaker worried over his statue, his attachment to it deepening with the passage of summer. When I went to the bathroom each evening to clean myself of grime I had to beat at the door for some time before he would come out. He had become more possessive of the figure and when he left his shrine he covered his totem with a cloth to protect it from other eyes.

The red-haired child came regularly to the stadium, and the three children investigated the place together, travelling its labyrinth of passages and stairways, and disappearing into its heart for whole days at a time. One afternoon I returned to find the three of them in the bathroom. The girl child was untying the cord that secured the cloth to the statue.

'Have you asked if you can do that?' I said. She pulled off the cover.

'This belongs to all of us,' she said. 'There's nothing else left of him.' Youth First turned to me.

'He was a sky-watcher,' he declared. 'And told stories in the language of the stars.'

'The language of his tribe,' I corrected him.

'It has its own music which is as important as the music of instruments,' he continued in a sing-song voice.

The girl child had lifted the carving from its alcove. She cradled it in her arms, and went into the main room. She set the figure down in the middle of the floor. It was about half as tall as her. Beside the black wood of the figure her skin looked very pale.

'We would like to borrow this,' she said. The caretaker had been away at the markets for some hours. He would not be back until afternoon. The children looked at me expectantly. I shrugged, and they picked up the figure and went down the steps to the waste-land. The emu called to them as they passed. I returned to the bathroom. Without the carving it looked empty, stripped of purpose. The tiles gleamed white. Although he neglected his own appearance, my father polished his shrine with unlimited energy. At intervals around the walls he had hung dried flowers, and on the shelf he had left a cloth stiff with his ejaculates.

I sat on the side of the bath and thought back over the period I had known my keeper, and of the changes I had witnessed. The growing strangeness of the man had an inevitability to it, as though confirming something I always suspected lay there in him, but which in part, at least, was the madness of the times. I recalled that distant summer day when we had first watched him from beneath the stand, the arc of his shovel and the regular shuffle of his boots. I thought of the contest of the trap, and of how having lost that battle, he had installed the device as one more prop on the stage of his derangement.

I remembered his voice in the stadium, the night he had sung there; the high, nasal tone, and my conviction that he was imitating something he had heard elsewhere. But I could no longer remember the tune of the anthem he had sung, and the more I tried to conjure it up, the further it receded from me. I sat there in the shrine for half an hour, searching for the melody. It would not come, and when I looked down, I saw that my hands were damp with sweat. I stood up quickly and went to the stadium.

At the ring, the children had left the carving in one corner, and were walking to and fro. As I came closer I could see they were involved in a game. I climbed the stairs to the place in the upper tiers where I had listened to the caretaker sing. I could recall that evening very clearly; the dip and swirl of the dancing lesson with my lover, the intoxication brought on by the fruit. The howl that had pierced the house. I remembered the echo of the caretaker's footsteps on the stairwell as he mounted the stadium to sing. But although I could recall the raw parody of the caretaker's voice from that night, the tune of the anthem was gone, and no matter how long I waited there it would not come back.

My father returned from the markets with a sack of ripened fruit. He said there was a glut of babaco and the produce had been dumped onto the city markets. In the evening we dined on the watery yellow fruit. The child cut her babaco into small cubes, carefully, and stabbed them with the end of her fork. Her black hair tumbled forward across her forehead as she ate, and the juice ran on her chin. I leaned over to wipe her face, and as I did so she gripped my wrist.

'Stop . . .' she forced my hand to the table with a crash '. . . that.'

I laughed, and heard the strange sound it made inside my head. I was surprised by her strength.

She released my wrist. 'Do you love me?' she said. I repeated the question to myself, trying to remember the last time I had heard the phrase outside a song. The green eyes in the china face considered me placidly. I found myself nodding, aware of the implausible movement of my head on my shoulders.

'You're my child,' I said. She began to impale the cubes of fruit. With her free hand she pushed the tangle of hair back from her forehead.

'How do you know?'

'I was there — at the birth.'

'So was he.' She waved at the caretaker with her fork. 'And he's not my father, is he?'

'I'm your god-father,' said the caretaker. He tapped his fingers on the table top. '*The sins of the god-father …*'

'Shut up'. The caretaker rubbed his chin as though I had struck him. He slid out of the chair and left the room. The child sat in silence. The cubes of babaco looked like pieces of flesh in her plate.

I motioned to the bathroom. 'He doesn't bring back as much as he did. I'll need help with the Christmas collecting.' She nodded, and began again to spear at her fruit with the fork.

We were given warning of the technicians' visit by Youth First, and some time after Christmas a covered vehicle crept up the drive. A number of women got down from the lorry and stood around with their hands in their pockets. They were clad in white cotton overalls, and wore their hair very short. The leader of the squad approached the house with a brisk walk. We met her on the veranda, and went to the store-rooms beneath the stadium, where the caretaker made some play of opening unlocked doors with his chain of keys.

The woman took papers from a brief-case and began to match entries on them against the equipment I had laid out for their inspection. I wondered whether the children had replaced everything they had borrowed. It seemed that the squad was only interested in the technical preparations, and the leader returned to the vehicle and motioned the driver to approach the stadium. The women moved with practised efficiency into the network of rooms beneath the stadium, examining the equipment and checking it for deterioration since the time of its first delivery.

The gang worked all day on the stadium, mounting television cameras on gantries high above the sand, running cable beneath the stands and fitting out a control centre with equipment from their truck. I watched them, noting their sure movements on the ladders, and the way they spoke among themselves in evenly modulated phrases. They worked in pairs, and did so with a familiarity that suggested they had been together for some time. When a technician stood at the bottom of a ladder she would know without speaking when to pass equipment to her partner at the top. The forewoman worked at the control room with a colleague, and did not appear to supervise her squad. Occasionally, if wanting access to a room that was still locked, or the use of the tractor, a member of the gang would come to the house — but they showed no curiosity in us, and their manner was distant and calm.

For five days the technicians worked on the stadium. Throughout the day and late into the night the area echoed with hammering and the sound of power tools. Great sweeps of cable ran around the stadium, and hung in festoons from its outer wall. More trucks arrived, and their wheels raised a column of dust around the stadium that mixed with the haze already hanging there, so that at times the arena seemed to be at the centre of a slow-moving dust storm. One vehicle carried the sections of a giant screen, which was mounted above the sand beside the north stand. Within a day, the technicians were sending patterns flashing across its face.

A marquee of green canvas was erected in the arena near the main entrance, and fitted with a long dining-table and chairs. Portable flower-beds were placed around the tent; and in front of this installation they set up parallel bars and a trapeze tower. Carpet was unrolled down the long concrete staircase that led to the ministerial box. On the last day they tested the public address system, and throughout the afternoon a metallic voice reverberated in the stadium, repeating in a monotone the same series of numbers, until I had to block out the sound by forcing my fingers in my ears.

Finally the technicians fixed banners among the stands: great sheets of cloth that hung limply in the stifling air, each marked with the insignia of the games.

During this period the child stayed away from the stadium, she showed little interest in the activities of the technicians. She spent most of her time amongst the palms, or in the kitchen, tracing her patterns on the grimy table, and singing to herself in a soft and breathless voice. The caretaker had bought new clothes for her at the market, including a dress of deepest blue, which she wore constantly, and would barely look at anything else. Occasionally she visited the emu, as the Aborigine had done before her, and sat just outside the circle of its claws, humming to it as to a friend and throwing it a handful of grain. Her friends did not appear while the technicians were present. When eventually the last of the trucks left and quiet returned to the stadium, I went with the child to look at the work that had been carried out.

We stood before the boxing ring, which had been draped in pale colours. The stadium was transformed. In five days it had become ready for spectacle, dressed and unrecognisable from the shell I had known for so long. Streamers flew from the balconies, and pillars had been hung with clusters of bright balloons. The child had insisted I bring the flute, and now she climbed up between the ropes of the ring. Although a technician had polished the surface until it shone, the dust had settled again as a light powder. A standard had been erected in each corner of the ring, from which ribbons moved slightly in the air-currents that circled the stadium floor.

The girl child leaned over the ropes towards me. For an instant, reflection from the surface of the ring made her face seem ancient, wise. She pointed to the instrument.

'Music,' she said. 'Play your flute.' Memory was a box of chiming puzzles, unpacking itself before me, and the chime of that particular memory was so clear in my head that I nearly fell. I was back on that summer night when my lover had taught me to dance, the scent of her fresh on the air. The ground under my feet seemed to be holding me steady while that pungent memory threatened to make me fall. The child was looking at me impatiently.

'I haven't played for months,' I said, weakly.

She plucked at her deep blue dress. The expression on her face in that moment was recognisable to me, the cast of her mother's face perhaps, or was it my own . . . ? She removed the obsidian blade from a pocket and turned it in her hand.

'Music,' she repeated. 'Play your flute.' She held the obsidian between finger and thumb, the way that someone might hold a razor. Was I on trial again? I watched the object in her hand, convinced for a moment that sentence, if pronounced on me, would be carried out with this very blade. The flute seemed cumbersome in my hands. I had a sudden desire to fling it into the sand. Instead I lifted it to my lips, but the metal was bitter on my mouth and I could not bring myself to sound the thing. I held out the flute to the child.

'You play it.' The child balanced the instrument carefully in her hands. She put her mouth to the embouchure hole and blew. The flute gave out a short, sour note. The child rearranged her lips over the mouthpiece and frowned in concentration. She blew again, the same harsh sound, and this time, despite the imperfection of the tone, something in the acoustics of the arena picked up the note so that it flew among the upper tiers of the stands in a train of muted echoes that went on and on.

'The place is listening,' she said.

'It's been listening for years.'

Looking around me at the stadium, fitted out in its ceremonial garb, hung with its decorations, I felt a little feverish. An obscure sense of propriety came over me. Hadn't I, after all, groomed the stadium in readiness for the coming events? Hadn't I carried and washed the sand through the suffocating heat of summer? Responsibility had passed gradually, through force of circumstance rather than design, from the caretaker to myself. I took a deep breath, inhaling the stadium air.

'This place is a kind of . . . museum,' I said. I was aware that I was addressing myself as much as the child. 'It's been standing here for decades, gathering the past around it. Witnessing the history of the nation.' I looked up at the ministerial box, vivid now in its drapes of red cloth. 'Think of the sights it's seen. The spectacles! Year in, year out, the population have come here to celebrate their way of life — to understand themselves. Places like this are a kind of monument to the nation. A museum of our history, but without exhibits.' I turned the phrase in my mind. 'A museum without exhibits,' I said more firmly.

I was surprised by my speech. The child had been watching me while I spoke. She had listened, I thought, with some care. I held out my hand for the flute, and extracted it from her grip. In recent months the balance between us had changed. She had acquired a different manner. More of the adult had emerged in her. But she was a child again now, a child with obscure games and insistent demands, but a child nevertheless. One day the history of our nation would become clearer to her. When the time was right I would try to explain a few things. I lifted her down from the ring, and we walked together across the arena, her fingers curled loosely inside my own.

141

Her friends were waiting on the veranda and stirred when we approached. Youth First was stretched out in a chair like an old man, his feet on the veranda rail. His orange bag lay across his stomach, and he fumbled inside it, perhaps for food. The other child stood beside him, graceful and quiet, her mass of red hair tied up with a bow. She looked down at me from the veranda.

'Tonight,' said the redhead in her reasonable voice, 'we want you to be our audience.'

'That would be an honour,' I said with a mock-formal bow. 'And what are you performing?' She sucked her bottom lip.

'We haven't decided that, yet. It will be a surprise, won't it?' She glanced at the girl child, then went on, 'We won't have to lock you up this time.'

'Thank you,' I said. 'I would prefer that.'

'In fact we may never have to lock you up again,' she said with a sudden, brilliant, smile.

I was led that night to my seat above the ring. The arena was illuminated by the banks of floodlights around the upper perimeter of the stadium. To begin with I was blinded: the light danced on metal and glass and seemed to penetrate the fabric of the place so thoroughly that the furniture of the stadium — plastic seats, hand-rails and pillars — became translucent and bled white at the edges.

When I had been seated, the redhead descended the stairs to the arena. She and the girl child now stood in the ring. For twenty minutes they remained poised there, until I began to shift in my seat with discomfort. Then Youth First appeared at the entrance to the stadium. He crossed the sand to join them. He was carrying a statue, as large as himself, which he manoeuvred between the ropes. The children moved it to the centre of the ring. These events took place directly below me, and the figures were clear beneath the powerful lights. The statue was a winged woman. She appeared to be made of unfinished plaster, but her wings, a little chipped at the edges, were painted gold.

A goddess, I thought, or an angel. One of the statue's arms was crossed against her breast, and the other was broken off at the elbow. The children stood before the angel for some time. They began then to circle the ring. Imperceptibly they increased their speed, until they were crossing the surface like dancers. The movement was something between a skip and a glide, and occasionally, in unison, they would take a long step that carried them across the floor of the ring like graceful flying creatures. At some invisible signal they stopped and reversed direction, their co-ordination faultless, and resumed their former movement. Now the dance became mesmeric, and I found myself bent forward in my seat, oblivious to all else, the rhythm of their steps and urgency of the spectacle drawing me in.

The statue stood at the centre of it all, her wings dull gold, her arm bent outwards in a gesture that was forever incomplete. Gradually the children slowed in their dance, until they had stopped altogether. They stood in the corners of the ring, waiting in silence, as if once more expecting a signal. But nothing came, and after a time I realised the performance was over, that my role of spectator was finished, and that I was expected to leave them to whatever came next. I got up from my seat and went down the gangway to the arena. The children did not acknowledge me on my way out.

That night the angel appeared in my dreams. She waited at the edge of a pool of light, her head inclined, out of sadness I thought, and I observed the coils of hair at her temple and the curve of her plaster neck. It was not the missing arm that troubled her, I was certain of that; it was something that I could not quite place — the burden, perhaps, of those flightless, plaster wings.

— 13 —

At breakfast I wanted to speak to the girl child of the spectacle, and of their angel. I guessed they had found her at one of the markets, where artefacts of previous times could be picked up cheaply, or at some ruined theatre in the city. The child ate her babaco, which floated in a bowl of milk, with the deliberation and care of a gourmet, and was silent throughout the meal. In the end I could not bring myself to speak of the spectacle. I asked instead when she expected her friends.

'It's their day off,' she said neutrally.

'And what do they do on their days off?' She looked up with an expression that suggested neither she nor I had the right to pry into the leisure activities of her associates.

Later, I went in search of the angel. I found her in a room beneath the stands. She lay in a wooden box, covered with a cloth, her arm protruding slightly above the rim. Since her return the dust had settled on her face. I cleaned off the grime with a handkerchief. At some stage her lips had been painted red, but the pigment had flaked to reveal a delicate pink. As in my dream, her expression was one of sadness, and the cold plaster of her skin conveyed distance and solitude. I replaced the cloth and left the angel to her silent room.

A few days after the performance in the ring, Youth First informed me that we were due another visit by the Guests. This was a last formality, it seemed, a final check that the technicians had prepared the stadium to their satisfaction. I suspected the caretaker would be in no shape to escort our visitors, but when I told him of the visit, he sat up stiffly at the table. His voice was urgent and strained.

'My duty is clear. And I have some free appointments this week.'

'All right,' I said. 'But you'll have to do something about your clothes.'

He touched the front of his shirt with his fingertips. His face worked briefly. He leaned forward, and I smelled the sourness of his breath. 'You know, I once held . . .'

I cut in, 'They'll want another batch of carvings.' He sat back, eying me reproachfully.

'They have more than they need. Anyway,' he said, 'there are other carvers, other sources.'

The caretaker shaved and washed his clothes as promised. I questioned him on the way he would deal with his visitors, and he seemed lucid enough in his intention to speak only when questions were asked of him, and to plead ignorance in the face of enquiries about casual callers to the stadium, should they arise. I thought it wise that he appear as the sole occupant of the place, I did not wish to repeat stories of relations on their way to the harvests. The morning of the inspection I took the child to our old space beneath the grandstand. I had not visited this place since the Aborigine's departure. All that remained of his occupation were a few scattered cans and the stump of a candle. The roof seemed lower and the place more claustrophobic than I remembered.

The girl child was silent and made no protest when I ushered her into the dark space. She curled up against the skirting. It was quiet there beneath the stands, and when after an hour or so I looked at the child, she seemed to be dozing, her chin tucked into her chest. Not so long afterwards, a vehicle turned into the drive and swept onwards towards the house. It slewed a little in the gravel before coming to a stop. Three Guests got out. I did not recognise the leader at first; his blond hair was longer now and tied back behind his head in a pony-tail. He was in shirt-sleeves, which he had rolled to the elbows and secured with a pair of clips.

The caretaker loitered on the veranda, and the leader acknowledged him with a nod as he passed. My father limped down the steps and followed them to the stadium. Beside me the child was still. I took her to be asleep. I crawled to a ventilation grill. Inside the arena the group made straight for the main stairwell, and climbed to the upper tiers, where they dispersed to examine the work of the technicians. They walked among the viewing boxes, inspected the flags and signalled to each other over some matter to do with their alignment. Eventually they descended to the arena to look at the equipment laid out there. Afterwards they disappeared into the green marquee, emerging, at last, to congregate in the ring. The blond-haired Guest made expansive movements with his arms. I could hear the murmur of their conversation. From this distance it seemed to me that they were pleased with how the stadium had been prepared, and were engaged in a round of self-congratulation. Affable but intent, the blond-haired leader gripped the elbow of each of his colleagues in turn, and they nodded and smiled at what he said.

All this time the caretaker waited near the gates, his hands thrust deep in his trouser pockets. Now the leader of the Guests beckoned to him. He approached them cautiously, his leg dragging a little as he walked. At an instruction from the leader, the caretaker climbed up into the ring and removed his boots and socks. He shuffled out into the centre. It was mid-afternoon, and the sun beat down on the metal and distorted the air above its surface. The caretaker lifted his feet like someone walking through tar, then began to leap from one foot to the other — a mincing, jerky dance. This continued for several minutes, while his movements became steadily more erratic. Eventually he lunged forward and rolled to a corner of the ring, where he lay curled against the ropes. The Guests helped him up and carried him to his boots. At this point the men lost interest in my father. They got down from the ring and wandered to the entrance, their heads bowed, while the leader explained something to his colleagues with rhythmic movements of his hands.

My father dragged himself up on the ropes and hung there like a beaten prize-fighter, shifting from one foot to another in agony. I crawled to the other side of the stand. Before long the Guests emerged from behind the curve of the stadium wall and made their way to the emu enclosure. They stopped just beyond the extent of the creature's leg rope. The bird let out a harsh cry, then ran to the end of its rope and lashed with its powerful claws at the visitors, who stepped back a pace. Again the Guests conferred, a joke of some kind, I thought, I could hear laughter in their voices. They turned then and walked to their vehicle, while the bird, its feathers fluffed out, screeched in a fury that continued long after the visitors had slammed the doors and driven away down the drive.

Seated on the edge of the bath that evening, his feet bathed in cool water, the caretaker told me that the Guests had been pleased with the state of the stadium. Festivities would begin in three days, he said. Administrative staff and cleaners had been allocated to the place for the term of the games, and his own duties would be limited to routine matters and to security work when other staff had left for the night. The emu was to be taken off our hands early. If the caretaker knew more than this he was not saying, and although I pressed him on the details of the spectacle, he examined his swollen feet and was silent. He had been correct about the carvings. Our visitors did not require any more of his figures. Existing stocks, it seemed, were adequate.

Above us in the alcove, the Aborigine watched with his thoughtful face. Condensation formed on the carving and ran in droplets to its base.

That evening I received an approach from the girl child. She stood at the kitchen door in her deep-blue dress, her hands folded before her. Her skin seemed transparent in the light of the kitchen. She cleared her throat. My presence at their performance was desired, she said, and her manner made this seem as much an instruction as a request.

When the noise of the city had subsided to the distant sound of trucks on the motorways, I took the path across the wasteland. Again the arena was lit, and the girls stood once more in the ring, their heads bowed. The place was set in deep silence. At an invisible signal, Youth First appeared at the entrance. This time he wore an animal head, and carried two more beneath his arms. He crossed the sand to the ring, where the children slipped on the masks. The performance began with a mechanical stroll, in which the children walked about the ring and brushed the ropes. The creatures kept their distance at first; each followed its solitary path around the ring. They had the distracted gait of animals in a zoo. Occasionally the creatures stopped in their march, looked up, and bayed silently at the floodlights overhead. With time, the pace of the masque increased, until the animals were stamping and pawing the ring. Often now they would collide, then rear up in anger and fear. Anarchy was loosed upon the ring, the creatures had become tormented by their confinement, and were searching for an escape. They ran against the ropes and staggered back in panic. Then one animal fell upon the other, and brought it to the floor. Struggling to free itself from the embrace, the victim writhed across the ring on its side, but the aggressor hung on, slashing at its prey, while round them the third beast danced a jig of predation and death. The creatures were maddened now, they were lost to their savage rite, they ran and bit and clawed each other in some silent battle zone of the soul. Throughout all this the statue of the angel stood in a corner of the ring, a still, neglected presence.

As suddenly the performance was over, and the animals were

back in their corners, motionless and heads bowed, as if waiting for applause. I tried to stand, but my legs would not move. I do not know how long I sat there, the passage of time lost all meaning and in the end it was the dimming of the lights that returned me to the present. The ring was now empty. I walked like a sleep-walker to the gates, and reached them a moment before the stadium was plunged into darkness.

The morning of the games dawned stiflingly hot. I had slept fitfully that night, drifting in and out of a sleep scarred by dreams. Drums woke me at first light, a faint but regular thump, and while I dressed I heard the skirl of pipes and the distant blare of brass. At times the music seemed to recede, but I guessed this was an illusion brought on by the laborious route the band was taking to the venue. The vehicle parks on the far side of the stadium began filling early, although the opening ceremony was not scheduled to start until midday. Arriving vehicles threw up more dust, so that the morning sun became obscured, and great elongated shadows moved across the stadium.

We were left alone at the house, the crowds that congregated outside the gates had no reason to come our way. I had heard from the caretaker that the games attracted a variety of marginals and hawkers who were excluded from the stadium, but who were tolerated amongst the queuing masses. In the presence of such crowds, I knew, there would be little attention paid to us. Half-way through the morning a murmur went up amongst the gathering spectators, and a line of vehicles appeared on a boundary road, their chrome-work gleaming, and swung into the main approach to the stadium. A pair of small flags flew stiffly from the leading machine. The crowd were subdued now, and stood quietly in the heat. Outside the main entrance the fleet came to a halt, and the passengers disembarked to be met by officials in the uniform of the Recreation Ministry. The party of Guests made their way to a side entrance. From there, I imagined, they would climb to their air-conditioned boxes to consume wines and other delicacies before the entertainment commenced.

The music was quite clear now, the band had entered the suburbs nearby. Amongst the clash of cymbals I could hear the sound of marching feet, and the insistent shrill of a whistle. By the window, the girl child pressed her face to the pane. Her breath misted the glass. I could not see her expression, only the curve of her cheek and the delicate line of her lashes. I watched the Guests file into the arena through a cordon of ministry officials, their fair heads bobbing amongst the crowd. Spectators were pushing at the cordon for a view, and the officials linked arms and leaned back against the throng. When the last of the Guests disappeared into the stadium, the cordon dissolved and officials mingled once more with the crowd. I left the child by the window and went out onto the veranda.

Official vendors had begun to move among the masses, smooth-faced youths with the poised look of those who exercise in gymnasiums — several dozen of them in all I guessed. They carried trays which hung from straps about their necks. A vendor came over to the technicians at the store-rooms, his call clearly audible above the milling voices of the crowd. I walked down the steps, crossed the waste-land and approached him, as a prospective customer might. He was no older than eighteen, and the tray about his neck caused him to move with a slight swagger. He rattled the thing as I came near. I saw then that it was packed with carvings, row upon row of them, their mad eyes and gaping mouths turned up to the sky. None of them had the mark of my father's knife — they were poorly cut and finished by comparison, the work of lesser craftsmen. I asked the vendor the price of his wares, and he glanced at me, briefly curious, before walking on without a word.

Although spectators poured through the turnstiles into the stadium, the crowd outside the entrance still grew. I had never seen such a mass of people, they came from the suburbs to the north, streaming down the road on the far side of the stadium in groups and loose-knit columns. They spoke quietly amongst themselves, with the suppressed enthusiasm of those unsure of what they are about to witness. A bus drew up in one of the parks and performers got out; clowns and vaudevillians in bright costumes. Some of the performers had thrown cloaks over their garb to disguise it from the crowds. Like the Guests before them, the new arrivals were spirited through the gathering masses to a side entrance.

On the stroke of midday a flight of aircraft passed overhead at great speed, three machines in tight formation, peeling outwards as they passed then circling to meet high above the city. The shock waves of their passage reverberated in the stadium for some time. I returned to the veranda of the house and watched the aircraft diminish to glints of light in the south. Inside the stadium now, the band struck up the national anthem, the tune that I had struggled to recall, and which now seemed so obvious that I could not explain how it had ever been lost to me. Gradually the crowd joined in, until the entire stadium was singing with one voice. As the anthem rose in the great well of the arena I felt suddenly hot and sick. I sat down in a chair beside the child. The sound engulfed us like some malevolent sea, many thousands of voices united in an anthem which spoke from the heart of the nation, that carried out over the roofs to the city, but whose words made no sense. At times, as one end of the stadium gained a few notes on the other, the anthem turned in on itself and became unrecognisable as music at all.

When the anthem had drawn to its close, a drum roll sounded, and was followed by lingering silence. Then a whisper began in the stadium and mounted in strength to a roar that seemed to physically take hold of the house. Glass in the windows vibrated with the force of the sound, and the contents of the cupboards rattled on their shelves. Outside, spectators still made their way towards the stadium entrance, the late-comers half-walking, half-running now in anticipation. The technicians had dispersed, and all that remained around the perimeter of the stadium were a few security officials and a lone vendor offering his wares to late-comers at the gates. I thought of trying to get to my old place beneath the stand, but abandoned the idea as too dangerous. Instead, I remained at the window and watched the last of the spectators push their way through the turnstiles. Again the sound of the crowd, and the noise when it came now was like the massive surging of water, or the rush of an irresistible wind.

Throughout the long afternoon of that first day the child and I sat listening at the window while the crowds voiced their enthusiasm for the events before them. Across the waste-land the emu waited in her enclosure, oblivious, it seemed, to the commotion. When they came for her, however — two animal handlers and a supervisor — the creature immediately sensed danger. She shrieked at the end of her leg rope, scattering sand and earth and slashing at the handlers with her claws. Eventually they threw a loop of rope around her neck and blinded her with a hood. Next they bound her legs and dragged her to a trolley, where she lay struggling on her side. The child watched the capture of the bird impassively, although at the moment the creature was finally taken away, she gripped the sill of the window more firmly with her small, strong hands.

The opening ceremony continued into the evening, when clouds accumulated overhead, the temperature dropped, and a storm, the first in months, blew in over the city. When the rain came it did so with sudden savagery, washing the dust from the air and covering the ground in a sheet of water. Security officials crouched in the lee of the stadium wall and shouted to each other above the sound of the deluge. At one stage a shallow lake formed around the stadium and I imagined that the performances inside had been halted. By the time the music of the band announced the end of festivities, and the spectators began to pour through the gates, the sky had cleared again, and sunset carved out deep shadows in the canyon of the stadium. The crowd were noiser now; they talked loudly amongst themselves and argued, I guessed, over aspects of their entertainment. They spread out from the gates in a fan, streaming back towards the suburbs to the north and east.

The Guests were the last to depart. They stood about in groups at the main entrance, surrounded by ministry officials and bathed in the luminous dusk. Their vehicles drew up, and gradually, as though reluctant to leave the venue, the Guests got into their limousines and were driven away into the northern suburbs. Later, when the last of the vehicles had left, floodlights lit up the area and gangs of cleaners began work. I went out to watch. Rubbish from the stadium lay everywhere, a stark battlefield beneath the lights. The ground had been churned up by thousands of feet, and was strewn with toy windmills, cardboard hats with the games insignia printed across their brims, and programmes made sodden from the downpour.

I could not bring myself to visit the arena, and returned to the house. With the first roar of the crowd the caretaker had retired to his shrine, and I found him now in that bright tiled room. He lay on the floor, his knees beneath his chin. His feet were bound with strips of cloth, which he had tied with clumsy bows, so that they looked like a pair of badly wrapped presents. He was humming an extract from the anthem, over and over again. Clutched to his breast was the statue of the Aborigine, and he held it against him with the strength of someone whose world is about to violently come apart.

14

Later that night, when the last of the debris had been carried from the stadium, and the cleaners had gone home, I was drawn back to the arena by the knowledge that, for me, the spectacle had only just begun.

At the centre of the ring, surrounded by her admirers, stood the muse. Her wings had been repainted by the children, so that the light fell golden and new from the feathers. When I had taken my seat in the stands, the children began their show, dipping and gliding across the floor, so graceful that they gave the illusion of creatures in flight. Slowly, the performers transformed their dance. Their performance took on other forms and spoke of stranger truths. Mysterious tableaux appeared before me, conjured from the air by the supple movement of the flying artists. They danced up the makers of myths and the leaders of strange rebellions. Populating that ring were the characters of stories unknown to me, stories that were half-finished and stories that had not yet been told. I saw the forgetful old and the reckless young, the musician and the actor, the collaborator and the seer. There were cripples and fools, saints and torturers; each took their place for a moment in a dance that reached out from the heart of that stadium and spoke to me of pasts that were to be fought over, and futures that were not yet formed. I was drawn into the performance against my will, again I forgot myself before the artistry of the dance.

And at the height of the performance I realised that I was no longer alone. In the stands below me sat two children I had never seen, crouched forward in their seats, as attentive to the ring as I was myself. The spell of the dance had entranced us all — the audience to that spectacle no longer watched in a place of sorrow at the heart of a decaying city — we sat together at some feast of the soul in which nothing was given and everything seemed possible. When, as before, the spectacle came abruptly to its close, my fellow spectators stood up, made their way to the stairs and disappeared into the darkness.

In my dreams that night a woman with a face of marble danced with a man of satin black; round and round they went, an endless circular jig, while at the edge of their pool of light, creatures of the night turned and walked, waiting for the light to dim.

A convoy of transports drew up at the stadium next morning, and were surrounded by officials before they had stopped. The transport drivers, surly, thin-faced men, stood together on the waste-land smoking cigarettes, and did not speak to the officials, as though having delivered their charges they wanted nothing more to do with them. The occupants of the transports got out, their movements stiff and awkward. Some were stooped, others limping. They had clearly been crammed together on the journey from their place of detention. They were led in single file to the rooms beneath the stadium. I recognised the Aborigine at once, the grace of his movements marked him out at once. His good arm lay across his chest in a sling. He wore his torn corduroy trousers and a pair of dusty leather sandals.

At the sound of the transports, the caretaker had emerged from the depths of the house, and stood watching beside me. Out on the steps, crouched against a veranda post and hugging her knees, sat the girl child. She had been there since first light, and I had been unable to persuade her to leave her vantage point. At the moment the Aborigine stepped down from the transport she turned her head and asked me without speaking a question for which I had no answer.

In order to screen the transportees from the crowds who had gathered for the day's entertainment, the vehicles had drawn up in a half-circle on the waste-land. Now the first of the detainees emerged from the store-rooms, dressed in the costumes prepared for them: elaborate outfits, designed, it seemed, to match the masks they carried beneath their arms. The Aborigine was amongst the last to be outfitted, and when he emerged he bore the mask of the minstrel nigger. At that moment he turned to look in the direction of the house, and I imagined I saw him raise his head to us in greeting . . . but then an official obscured my view of him and I was uncertain that he had seen us at all. He was taken like the others to the players' entrance, an escort at each elbow, the hem of his costume trailing on the ground. We watched until he disappeared from view.

As on the first day, festivities started at midday. Events began with a booming announcement that was unintelligible in the house because of the confusion of echoes it set off. The air had been washed of dust by the previous day's downpour, and for the first time in weeks the sun shone in a clear sky. Balloons were released in the arena, a thousand points of red, yellow and green, drifting on the breeze like a cloud of confetti, and a little later a flock of doves was set free. For some reason the creatures were unable to fly properly, and darted amongst the balloons with flailing wings and panicky swoops. Some of the birds managed to hurdle the stadium wall, and cartwheeled across the waste-land until they came to rest as quivering clumps of feathers in the dust.

Overhead the balloons hung suspended beneath a canopy of blue, forming and reforming in multi-coloured swarms.

The roar of the crowd, when it began, was more urgent and attentive than on the day before. I had insisted the child go indoors at the first echoing announcement. I wished now that I had followed her. I closed my eyes and felt the sun beat down on my head. Nausea rose again in my stomach. I was paralysed by the new sounds that came from the arena . . . unnameable sounds, echoes of the violent day-dreams that had tormented me through a dead season in an abattoir on a plain by a river many years before. Unthinkable images formed in my mind . . . spectres that I could not throw off. I was trapped by a performance that I could not see, caught up in the games I had helped prepare, and that I knew could now ensnare me as easily as they had the Aborigine. With the exaggerated clarity of fever, I saw a lone balloon, driven by the breeze, descend over the house and drift across the waste-land, until it burst against the hub-cap of one of the transports. I had begun to shiver despite the heat, and my clothes were damp with perspiration. A weight pressed down on my skull. With time the sound of the spectacle began to recede, until I was alone in a place of my own, and the stadium became a distant location, beyond the boundaries of my intensifying world of silence. Light followed shadow with a massive slowness across the veranda that afternoon, marking out the passage of the day — a day that carved itself into my memory with the indelible image of a white and mutilated bird, struggling on its back in the sand beneath an unforgiving sun.

I do not know how long I sat there in half-conscious witness of the rites taking place in the arena. I do know, however, that later that afternoon, when events were coming to an end, and birds had begun to gather in clouds above the stadium, the caretaker ran from the house shaking blood from a wound in his head. In a new gesture of penance, he had shaved his head so close to the bone that he had cut it open, and the pain had driven him from his shrine. A towel encased his head to stem the flow of blood. He passed me on the veranda, whispering, like a murderer leaving the scene of the crime. He ran among the palms in the garden, then sat down and rocked in silence, his head in his hands.

That night I lay on my bed in a sweat that ran from my pores and soaked the mattress. My tongue was swollen and raw. I did not know whether I had been scorched by the sun, or had contracted some illness. The children would be at the ring by now, preparing their own performance in an empty stadium, but I could no more get up and walk to the arena than I could resist the images that ran in my fevered mind. I saw the transport drivers in their taciturn circle, waiting to be gone. I saw the Aborigine, the mask beneath his arm, turn and nod gravely to those who had given him sanctuary. And I saw the knot of birds that appeared at the end of the day, their cries harsh above the babble of the departing crowd — the cawing of abattoir crows, or of birds that hunt in the dark.

Throughout that night and for the next two nights the fever kept hold of me, so that the events that played in the stadium and the games that took place in my head were indistinguishable from each other, and the cries and whispers became one blurred voice that rose from the depths of my delirious brain.

Occasionally I saw the lunar face of the girl child at my side, or the new-risen moon that shone through the window by my bed. In rare moments of clarity, I heard the sound of vehicles on the waste-land outside, their ceaseless manoeuvring beside the player entrances and the shouts of the marshals who directed them. Once I heard the mad baying of river dogs as they were transferred from waiting vehicles to the stadium. At other times the noise of the crowd was so intense that I was convinced the room I lay in had been transported to the stadium floor, and the spectacle took place a few feet from my head.

I emerged slowly from the fever. On the third day I was able to sit on the edge of my bed. After a time I went through to the kitchen for water. A weak sun shone through high cloud and the air outside was warm. There were no vehicles in the parks. The arena was quiet.

A poster at the stadium stated that the day had been designated free of games. Smaller print informed me that festivities would recommence in the morning and proceed for another eight days. I made my way through the turnstiles. Flags rippled in the breeze, and a few cicadas sang in the stands. The faint scent of previous summers hung there now; an odour that seemed at times to be undetectable, then caught at the back of the throat.

Deep shade enveloped the stands: I could not see whether the children played there. I called, and the echoes of my weakened voice rebounded amongst the endless staircases. There was no reply, and eventually I returned to the house. My father was at the kitchen table, arranging briar roses in a vase. For a moment I thought that the events of the last few days had returned him to some kind of calm, but when he turned to me I found myself gazing into the juvenile eyes of the irretrievably insane. The flowers clasped before him, and the statue of the Aborigine tucked under his arm, he stumbled away towards the stadium.

I took one of the last cans of toheroa soup from the cupboard, heated the pale liquid, and sat down to eat my first meal in days. The can had begun to corrode, the soup was sour and thin and coated my tongue and lips with its taste. I pushed away the plate and went out into the garden, which had been revived by the downpour of the previous week. The leaves of the palms seemed brighter, the foliage more lush. I sat down under the avocado. Attached to the tree was the chain I had once used to tether my father, now rusted and broken. A few fruit hung on the branches. Birds had attacked the avocados, and flesh leaked from the wounds. I took a fruit from the tree, tore at the leathery shell with my teeth and sucked on the pulp.

The games had receded from me now. They occupied a dimension that I had left behind, and the taste of the fruit intensified my sense of having returned to a different present. When I looked across the waste-land to the concrete structure beyond, it seemed to me that the place had remained unused and empty for many years. I must have dozed off there beneath the avocado, because I woke some time later to the pressure of a bicycle tyre against my ankle. The sun had settled behind the palms, and the garden was steeped in aquatic light. A breeze stirred the leaves of the tree. Above me stood the children. At the edge of the garden waited two more children, whom I recognised as my fellow spectators from the other night.

The redhead squatted at my feet. She rocked a little as she observed me, and tucked a wisp of hair behind her ear. Beside her, Youth First leaned on his bicycle. He was stroking the machine, absently, as a rider might caress a horse. The girl child stood between them, very still, watching me with her unwavering gaze.

'Tonight . . .' began the redhead.

'You're giving a performance,' I said, struggling to sit up. 'And you want me to be your audience.'

The redhead leaned forward. There was no trace of her previous good humour. She shook her head.

'We want you to be the narrator.'

Insects hummed among the branches of the avocado. Out across the city, lights flicked on, touching the skyline with points of brightness. The mountains had withdrawn into a grey-blue mass, without contour or detail. In the kitchen, the caretaker was preparing food, and the sound of his movements carried across the garden, amplified by the stillness of the dusk. Youth First spun the pedal of his bicycle and fiddled with his bell.

I got to my feet, unsteadily. *'But I don't know the story.'*

The girl child laid her hand on my arm. Her touch was cool and dry. She watched me from beneath fine black lashes. In the shadow of the garden, I was unable to pick her exact expression. I do not know how long we stood there in the gathering twilight, father and child, locked in a moment that seemed to stretch on and on, but later, as she led me with the children towards the lights of the stadium, I marked that look as the ancient ambiguous gaze of the poet, the seer, the dancer.

160

The children stood around their muse. After a pause, the motion began, the newcomers taking their places like experienced performers, the movement of the children so languorous that it was possible once more to believe that they glided above the metal surface. They no longer wore masks, and the gentle opening gave way to a faster tempo. A spectacle of passion began to unfold, the movements intense and sinuous, the performers driven by a force more powerful than themselves. The play spoke now of suffering and loss, of innocence and faith, of fallen priests and transcending angels. It told of the blighted years, of empty halls and abandoned theatres, of official truths and partial histories, of a crabbed and listless populace. And it spoke of the crucible of performance, the refuge and mystery of the dance, and of the struggle to carve out form from the chaos of the times. At the centre of it all, aloof in her beauty, stood the statue, a figure the dancers reached out to but could not touch.

The dance then moved to a close; not suddenly as before, but with a gradual slowing of movement, until the children came to a halt before the angel.

At that moment they raised their eyes to where I sat. I looked at the flags around the stadium, their insignia sharp beneath the floodlights. To my right the windows of the ministerial box had been slid back, and the dark womb of its interior was lit up. Binoculars and chairs were set out in preparation. Glasses stood on a shelf, a row of bright crystal. The children were motionless, fixed in the glare of lights. I felt their unrelenting gaze. The scent of the arena rose from the sand, hot and thin in my throat. I stood, abruptly. The lights of the stadium were brighter now, and behind them I could see dark forms, hard eyes, the hidden faces of interrogators. Shapes began to distort. I saw an odd-sided building, a cell of dreamy liquid, and a storm of blood-coloured flakes. Below me, the children were still, a tableau of illuminated figures. I stumbled to the aisle and down the steps.

I ran out into the arena, and felt the sand, soft and treacherous, beneath my feet. I ran past the ring (I did not look up) and towards the gates, the blood surging in my head. Across the waste-land, past the house and out into the drive, the gravel beneath my feet, the night like a blade in my lungs. Banana palms swayed as I passed. The sky was an abyss from which the stars of the southern night burned down, a vault of purple-black. I entered the industrial suburbs, and familiar buildings emerged from the darkness, buildings that I had passed on my last visit here, great structures that lay behind high gates and bright wire. I ran faster, the echoes of my footsteps bounding among warehouse walls. I passed shop-fronts, derelict vehicles, the place where a pair of spectacles had glared up at me with the fury of unrecorded injury. I passed the warehouse I had visited long before, its floodlights turning my shadow to four fleeting ghosts. Behind me a guard-dog began to bark, but the sound faded as I plunged on through the night.

The streets were strange to me now, the facades of buildings unfamiliar. I had entered a different zone, in which the structures were signless, their purpose too obscure or too important to be noted on their exteriors. I passed rows of concrete silos, street upon street of them, indistinguishable from each other. I passed long sheds, their facades windowless and without visible means of entry. I ran on through the city . . . down narrowing streets, across vacant lots, and along alleys between buildings when barred by the blind walls of cul-de-sacs. After a time the warehouses began to thin out, the open spaces became more frequent, and I knew then that I was approaching the slow river to the east. The smell of that place grew stronger, the scent of mangrove and half-drained swamp, a cool odour that I craved after the sickly scents of the stadium. Eventually I came to the bank of the river, and lay down amongst the reeds. At some time during my flight from the stadium the pain in my lungs had eased. A moon had risen and cast angled light on the water. Amongst the sound of marsh frogs, and the sigh of the midnight wind in the reeds, I lay with my cheek against the mud of the bank and slept.

If creatures of the river came near me, I did not know it, I was oblivious to their movements. I spent that night in dreams of distant places. I dreamt of a sea of calmest blue, of circling gulls and pure horizons. And I dreamt of the endless plains of the south, of clear bright streams, and of lying with my languid, loose-limbed lover beneath an apricot tree that bent with the burden of a crop that had never been picked.

·•

15

I came to that river at the end of the summer, and made my home amongst the marshes. In the mornings I lay amongst the reeds and watched the sun cast shadow beneath the mangroves, or thought of how to exorcise the arena, which rested, I now knew, in my soul, although I was uncertain of how this had come about. At times I believed the cool squalor of the swamps, their night sounds and insinuating smells, might cure me of that distant place, but at other times I was convinced that I was lost to the stadium, that I had become irrevocably marked by its curse.

In the afternoons I watched the slicks on the river move with silent speed towards the sea, and in the evenings I fed on jewel-green frogs and the sweet stems of marsh-shrubs. At night, in my dreams, I followed the route-ways of my travelling years, often alone, sometimes with my lover, trying to trace the paths that had led me to that labyrinth at the heart of the city. Under the canopy of those straggling mangroves I recalled the day that my lover had discovered the tiled bathroom, and of bathing her with a fine hard spray. I remembered our early trips for food, of an appetite that would not be sated, and of the grease and salt of mutton-bird flesh.

In the evening, guided by an intermittent moon, I followed the tracks among the marshes. I caught flounder in the shallows and took swamp-bird eggs from beds of flattened reeds. Often, on those walks, I saw the silhouettes of dogs on the river-bank paths, but none of them came near, although I sensed on occasion that they followed me for hours before disappearing into the darkness. It was cooler beside the river than in the house by the stadium, and when I slept I covered myself with reeds. In the early hours I would wake and listen to the world, the stirring of its distant life. The range of sounds was different now, I could no longer hear the murmur of city traffic, which had been replaced by the moist, tenacious sounds of the river.

I saw no one along that waterway, although evidence of the city floated by . . . a child's wooden cot . . . bright dye-stains from the factories . . . great rafts of rotting fruit. One afternoon I found a boat among the reeds, its woodwork freshly painted, separated from some distant mooring by a storm, I guessed, and delivered to me complete with oars. There was lettering along its prow, an identification code of sorts. I dragged the craft to the bank. At night I lay beneath its hull and dreamed of rowing to the sea, of hugging the beaches and headlands, of a cautious route to the south. But as soon as I launched the boat it opened a leak, and when I beached the craft and scraped at the bright new paint, I found it carious with worm, as if someone had plotted my drowning.

That afternoon I took off my clothes and waded into the river. The arrangement of shoals caused the water to swirl and shift. I moved out into the stream with a steady crawl. Thirty metres from the shore, the river became shallow again. I touched bottom with my feet, and stood up on a mud-bank. Far upstream I could see the place where the river began to narrow between low banks and overhanging trees. Downstream it widened into a brown expanse, hemmed by the marshes.

A pair of large birds flew low over the water, their feet skimming the surface, then settled in the fast-moving centre channel. I watched them hunt for fish, diving beneath the current, then drying their feathers in a delicate shimmy. The larger of the birds took off again down-river, a writhing shape in its beak. I waded across to the centre channel. The water moved swiftly by, and unlike the water in the side-channels, it was a pure unclouded green. Anything that entered that channel would be carried for miles, the speed of the current would see to that. A torpor came over my limbs. I imagined sliding into its depths, following its route to the sea. I stood there a long time, hypnotised by the sheet of moving water. At last I turned away, waded across the mud-bank and struck out through the side-channels for the shore.

From my home in the swamps I could see the upper stands of another stadium, a sister to the one I had abandoned, and beyond, the buildings of the central city area. At dawn each day, I watched these structures form on the horizon, and tried to imagine them filling with a population drawn in from the far-flung suburbs. As the sun rose overhead, a layer of foul air gathered above these buildings, almost touching their highest points. Sometimes I convinced myself this cut-out city was real, inhabited by bustling urban masses, but for most of the time it was merely a cluster of two-dimensional shapes on the skyline. At dusk, the setting sun caught the glass in the highest of the buildings and lit the darkening marshes with a sudden blaze of light.

On the other border of the marshes the southern suburbs began, and in my walks I sometimes came to this zone; endless streets of wooden houses, unkempt lawns and broken blinds. I knew this area stretched for many miles, and had considered trying to traverse the region as the Aborigine had attempted before me, but abandoned the idea on the grounds that I would stand out too obviously amongst the populace. Instead, under cover of the darkness, I ventured into the margins of these suburbs in search of food, filing through pitted streets and empty lots, rousing the curs that slept in dingy yards, then returning to the swamps where I knew that I would be unlikely to be pursued.

During my time in the marsh, I crossed it many times, and

eventually few of its backwaters were unknown to me. I walked that place with the resolution of the pursued. Each night I fell asleep beneath my rotting hulk in the hope that exhaustion would dull the edge of my dreams. But the stadium would not leave me, I could not get it out of my head. I saw it in my reveries, in my nightmares, in the reflected sunsets of the river. I watched the dawn light up its sister to the north. I heard the singing of a crowd in the sighing of swamp winds, and in the wash of tidal flows. Wherever I went in that wilderness of marsh and water, I carried the arena with me, it had seared itself into my brain.

A week and one day after I arrived in the swamps I took my worm-ridden shelter and pushed it out from the bank. The boat moved sluggishly at first, then swung to face the current. Eventually it was drawn to the centre channel, and from there it accelerated towards the sea, settling as it went. I watched until it disappeared beyond a bend, then turned my back on the river and set out for the western edge of the marshes. Three hours later I entered the industrial zone. By daylight, the warehouses looked bland, colourless. I could make no connection between the area and the cityscape I had fled through eight long days before. I walked for an hour, and saw no one at all. A fine dust had settled on streets and pavements, as though the place had been undisturbed for years. Blind windows, steel doors, derelict fire-escapes: the furniture of a zone that by day was asleep, but by night would have a busy, ordered life of its own. In an alley-way between warehouses I saw a cardboard shelter and ash from a cooking fire. Beside it were the rinds of half-eaten fruit, but there was no sign of the vagrants who had sheltered there. I walked on, retracing the route I had taken in my flight from the stadium, as the sun beat down and the heat rose from the surface of the street. Occasionally, as I passed a warehouse, the odour of ripe produce would flood the air, and I covered my face to escape its cloying scent.

I came to the place where the road ended and a foot-bridge spanned an area of marshalling yards, a legacy of the time that railways had serviced the zone. The piers of the bridge were covered with yellow lichen. Nearby a signal-house looked out over empty yards, an expanse of rusted tracks and run-down sheds. Weeds grew beside the rails and choked the sidings, so that the place resembled a massive untended garden. I had come to the final stage of my journey. Beyond the railway yards, the street rose towards the stadium. I sat down to rest in the shade of the bridge and traced with my eye the network of trunk lines and sidings. I tried to picture the yards as they must once have been, busy with trains and watched over by attentive men in buildings high above the tracks; but the past had become a far-off country that was harder to imagine with each passing day.

By the time I started across the foot-bridge the sun was lower in the sky. The day had cooled. I made good time, and within an hour the buildings around me had become recognisable. Occasionally now I could see the upper tiers of the stadium between obscuring warehouses. It was late afternoon by the time I approached the house. I took the cautious route I had followed so long before when my lover and I had observed the caretaker from amongst the palms. From the edge of the garden the place seemed quiet.

I made my way to the back steps and climbed to the veranda. The creak of its boards was very loud. Inside, all was still. I went through to the kitchen. The cupboards were stocked with food and the floor had been recently swept. After the open spaces of the swamps the house seemed small and cramped. In the bedroom I stared at the wall. The picture of the woman in red had been removed. The square of wallpaper where it had hung stood out from the surrounding faded pattern. It occurred to me, irrelevantly, that in all my time in the house, I had never noticed the design of the wallpaper before. I opened the window. A gust of warm wind filtered through the house, stirring the curtains and the pages of open books. The house seemed to be asleep. Outside, the shadow of the stadium lay inert on the waste-land. I knew from the calendar I had kept in the swamps that the season had finished today. In the three or four hours since festivities had ceased, the cleaners had almost completed their task. A few streamers blew towards the road. The parks were empty of all but a handful of cars; the vehicles, I guessed, of cleaning staff. There was no sign of the children. I left the house and walked to the stadium. As I approached, I could sense the heat of the day in the massive concrete walls.

The turnstiles had been swung back to allow the passage of the departing crowds. Posters had been torn down, and shutters raised in the ticket booths. I walked through the gates. To my right stood the green marquee, surrounded by flower-beds. Before me, the arena spread out in a plain, the sand now marked by thousands of feet. At the far end of the stadium the ring lay abandoned, its decorations not yet removed by the technicians. The place seemed locked in silence — a limpid dream of past spectacles that would stretch out now for another year.

I walked to the centre of the arena, my feet scuffing the sand, and looked up at the galleries and the lines of undulating flags. Only a few hours before, the climax of the games had taken place here, a closing ceremony that would have silenced the watching masses with its grandeur. As I stood there beneath the ministerial box, I became aware of a murmur that rose and fell with time. The acoustics of the place made it difficult to locate the sound, a distant mutter that I thought at times I imagined. Several minutes elapsed before I realised that the sound originated at the level of the arena floor, and that it was the sound of conversation. I turned to the marquee. The tent stood fifty metres away, and was supported by fine nylon ropes, each secured to a stake driven deep in the sand. Around it, flower-beds had wilted in the heat. The murmur came from inside, I was sure of that. I waited to see whether the occupants would emerge, but although the canvas rippled and stirred as the walls were brushed from within, no one came near the entrance. After a period of silence, the conversation resumed, and was punctuated by a scattering of applause.

I walked slowly across the arena. I was aware of a metallic taste on my tongue, as though the fillings in my teeth had begun to dissolve. I swallowed, my mouth dry and the taste of mercury in my throat. I stopped at the entrance to the marquee. The conversation was louder, and I was able to pick out the occasional phrase. Then a laugh flared amongst the murmur of voices, a laugh that reached out from the interior of that tent and cut me with the precision of a surgical instrument. I was conscious of the slowing of time, and of the sensation of blood draining from my head. I stared at the sand. Each particle had become very clear. I studied the variety of shape and colour among the grains, their precise position in relation to each other, and thought how strange it was that they had been so carefully arranged for my observation. I lifted the flap of the tent and looked inside

At a table in the centre of the marquee sat a party of Guests. Before them stood a rose and candlesticks. The hands of the diners were soft and perfectly formed, and they stripped the flesh from the food they ate with the elegance of the elect. Beside them sat my lover, Jan, expensively dressed, with the fragile intensity of the reclaimed. Her lips were red, and her hair was arranged on her head in the manner of those who attend grand spectacles. A last supper, I thought, but a supper set to outlast any other last supper. The diners near me turned their heads and wiped their moistened mouths. Their conversation slowly hushed. Formless eyes met mine. In that expanded moment of terror, my past and the past of the nation telescoped into one. I saw clearly, and almost understood, the intractable truth of the times, the predatory pasts that are half-dead but rise again to reclaim you, and the inescapable lure of our masters. It was clear to me then that the caretaker had invoked Jan's origins in the families that had welcomed the Guests, that she had been drawn back into her lost history, that this was a time of mystery and great loss, where relationships died in the thin soil of our emaciated pasts, and that those who sought to escape their history did so briefly, their lives pitched only temporarily in freedom.

I saw then the struggle to wrest new stories from the times, and I felt the inevitability of defeat. I cried out in a voice I did not know, a howl that rose in my gut and voided its blackness in the arena. It took me and tore at me until it seemed to shred every last nerve in my brain, and it was the howl of a sulphur train on a curve above the sea . . . of a bloody birth on a distant autumn morning . . . of abandoned clothes in a scented sandal-wood box. And then a Guest was rising from the table and walking with calm steps towards me. He drew back his hand with something flexible arched there and struck me on the neck, and again so that for a moment of firmly curled time I saw my own blood spray outwards at him and wet his clothing, a convincing fan of it, I thought. I was on the verge of an apology, when the moment adjusted itself to accommodate a pain that was so intense and yet external that I gave in to its outsideness with relief.

Not so long afterwards, I became conscious that a Guest was bending over me. I told him that I didn't like his teeth. 'They're too white,' I said, and could hear that my voice sounded fluted and unstable. He continued to look down at me with a distant curiosity, until I slipped away again into darkness, a sombre night that contained its own very special visitors and guests.

I woke in a windowless room with the stale scent of urine on my clothes. I was aware of pain from several parts of my body, including my skull. I put my hand to my head and felt a wound that ran from temple to chin, and which was crusted with blood. For a while I lay on the floor, submitting to a pain that came in waves. Eventually I sat up. My surroundings moved briefly into focus. The room was a bare cell, its walls painted white. From the angle of light through the open door I guessed it to be late afternoon. Pinned to my shirt was a piece of card that I had to peer at to read. On one side was the logo of the Ministry of Recreation. On the other was hand-printed: 'MARGINALS EXCLUDED FROM THIS VENUE.' I got up awkwardly, and walked to the door. The room opened out onto a familiar stretch of sand. I was no more than a hundred metres from where I had been struck down. I waited there, squinting at the arena, until my eyes had adjusted to the light. In the time I had been unconscious, the stadium had been stripped of its decorations. The green marquee was gone.

I stepped out onto the sand, and the stadium dipped and wheeled. When my head had cleared, I took another step. Overhead, clouds moved across a sky of egg-shell blue. Sunlight fell on the sand as on an ocean floor, patches of light that formed and subtly reformed. Above me in the stands I saw the flicker of a moving figure, and as I made my way out into the arena, a drone became audible, the sound of my father's voice. I saw him then on a walkway, shuffling along like a blind man, the statue held close to his chest. I watched him limp through the tiers, sealed in the world of his madness, one hand gesturing to an invisible companion, until he was swallowed up in the northern stand. I stood there for a while, my eyes on the spot where he had disappeared. I considered setting out after him, dragging him to the upper tier, and throwing him over the rails. Instead, I walked to the end of the stadium and looked at the place where the marquee had stood. There, I knelt down in the warm sand and wept.

Some time later, I was conscious that the children stood around me. They had approached so silently that I was unaware of their presence until the girl child cleared her throat. She wore her deep-blue dress, and was a little more dirty than when I had seen her last. Her companions stood nearby, a pair of watchful aides. Youth First stroked his arm, and gazed at my wound with interest. I had never seen him without his message bag before. The redhead carried a bowl of water in one hand, and a piece of cloth in the other. She was dressed in a party frock with a torn, organza skirt — scavenged, I guessed, from the refuse sacks of a distant suburb. She bent to her knees, wet the cloth, then began to clean the cut in my head. As her hair brushed my face, I caught her girlish scent, some cheap perfume from the markets. When she dipped the cloth in the bowl, the water bloomed a sudden red.

The girl child watched with a careful, searching look. While her companion cleaned my wound, I listened to my slowing pulse. The touch of the cloth, the trickle of lukewarm water, and the silent watching children obscured the passage of time, so that when at last I looked at the redhead, I was unable to tell whether she had been at work for minutes or hours. Eventually she stepped back, inspected her handiwork and emptied the bowl in the sand. The pain had gone now, and I felt calm and more clear. I gazed around me at the stadium. The tiers of seats were picked out with greater clarity than before. The stadium appeared neutral, resting, as though waiting to take on the character of whatever should occur here.

One day we would get away from this place, the children and I, and I would show them rivers, open fields, a wide pacific sea. But for now, the stadium was our home. I looked again at my attendants, standing around me in a half-circle, lost in their solemn thoughts. I could tell that although the games were over for another year, there would be no halt in their own performance. The angel was waiting, the dances had only just begun. The girl child's green, wide-set eyes met mine. Poised there was the question that had been put to me twice, the invitation that had pursued me to the swamps and had haunted my dreams. And as the wind blew sand in flurries across the arena, and brought to that place the scent of end-of-summer orchards, I reached out to the small white hand of this dancer, my daughter, and told her, Yes.

A Selected List of Fiction Available from Minerva

While every effort is made to keep prices low, it is sometimes necessary to increase prices at short notice.
Mandarin Paperbacks reserves the right to show new retail prices on covers which may differ from those
previously advertised in the text or elsewhere.

The prices shown below were correct at the time of going to press.

☐ 7493 9026 3	**I Pass Like Night**	Jonathan Ames	£3.99
☐ 7493 9121 9	**Evening Wolves**	Joan Chase	£5.99
☐ 7493 9808 6	**To Kill a Mockingbird**	Harper Lee	£5.99
☐ 7493 9907 4	**Pinocchio in Venice**	Robert Coover	£5.99
☐ 7493 9046 8	**Love in the Days of Rage**	Lawrence Ferlinghetti	£3.99
☐ 7493 9027 1	**The Lover of Horses**	Tess Gallagher	£3.99
☐ 7493 9032 8	**Years From Now**	Gary Glickman	£4.99
☐ 7493 9189 8	**Paper Products**	James Hall	£5.99
☐ 7493 9099 9	**The Sporting Club**	Thomas McGuane	£4.99
☐ 7493 9132 4	**Bicycle Days**	John Burnham Schwartz	£4.99
☐ 7493 9072 7	**Leaving Brooklyn**	Lynne Sharon Schwartz	£4.99
☐ 7493 9957 0	**The Joy Luck Club**	Amy Tan	£5.99
☐ 7493 9141 3	**Vineland**	Thomas Pynchon	£4.99
☐ 7493 9155 3	**Grapes of Wrath**	John Steinbeck	£5.99

All these books are available at your bookshop or newsagent, or can be ordered direct from the publisher.
Just tick the titles you want and fill in the form below.

Mandarin Paperbacks, Cash Sales Department, PO Box 11, Falmouth, Cornwall TR10 9EN.

Please send cheque or postal order, no currency, for purchase price quoted and allow the following for
postage and packing:

UK including
BFPO
£1.00 for the first book, 50p for the second and 30p for each additional book ordered
to a maximum charge of £3.00.

Overseas
including Eire
£2 for the first book, £1.00 for the second and 50p for each additional book thereafter.

NAME (Block letters) ....

ADDRESS ....

....

☐ I enclose my remittance for ....

☐ I wish to pay by Access/Visa Card Number

Expiry Date